Vícious

PLEASURE & PREY

AJ MERLIN

D1704595

Vicious

Cover Design by Books & Moods

Paperback isbn: 978-1-955540-28-5

*This book is a dark romance, and there are some aspects that may not be for all readers. **Vicious** contains scenes of dubious consent, kidnap, mention of assault and abuse (though nothing on page) and questionable kinks such as somnophilia, kidnap, CNC, and more.*

ONE

Of course I'll help you.

The memory of his hands cupping my cheeks, of the look in his warm brown eyes, isn't enough to tear my attention from the diner.

It isn't enough to make any of this go away.

My hands shake as I let the door close behind me, eyes fixed on the blood that's sprayed up the wall behind the bar of the fifties-themed diner. Music still plays through the jukebox, and when I turn to look at the lit up display of its old-timey front, I see that it's one of the few things in the building not marred by blood.

You can trust me.

Whistling, constantly whistling. Dr. Gabriel Brooks is always whistling whenever I walk into his office until he turns and sees me. Then he smiles and remarks about me being a breath of fresh air compared to the other patients he'd taken over from Springwood Medical.

I just like to whistle, he'd told me, mouth curved into the sweetest smile as the smile-lines around his eyes had deepened. *Is it weird?*

I'd just assumed my new therapist was bullshitting me about being his favorite patient. Until this morning.

Until now.

My hands shake as I round the counter, eyes pinned to the shape on the floor. Marcie Owens, her blonde hair tangled and matted with blood, had owned the diner with her husband, Frank. Neither of them were particularly great people, and they'd raised a son with just as much entitlement and arrogance as them.

They'd always been out of place in Springwood.

What's wrong? He'd caught me when I came into his office, sobbing, with blood on my hands and feeling light-headed. *Just tell me what's wrong, Quinn. You can tell me.*

I had. I'd told him everything. Like a good therapist, he'd gotten the story from me without me even realizing he was asking for more details than I'd wanted to give.

I'd been so afraid, so terrified after what had happened. It wasn't *my fault,* but no one else would see it that way. My fault or not, I'd be kicked out of my scholarship program because of it. I'd end up on the street, instead of on my way to college. Being eighteen meant that foster care didn't give a damn anymore.

I'd be alone, even if it wasn't *my fault.*

He'd told me that he'd take care of it, and I'd thought my therapist would just appeal to someone. I'd thought he'd bring in Billy Owens' parents and talk things out with them.

I'd thought that everything would be *okay.*

I kneel beside Marcie, my shaking hand reaching out before coming to a stop just over her face. With her eyes open wide with fear, I find it hard to tear my gaze away from her. Nausea rolls in my stomach, and finally I get to my feet, unable to stay down here with her body in its dried pool of blood any longer.

Marcie Owens is dead, and there's nothing I can do about it.

My steps take me further into the diner, even though I have a good feeling about what I'll find. If Marcie is dead and the place is silent, then there has to be only one answer.

When I find the body, though, I wish I hadn't. I step back, shoes slipping on the wet floor as a wretched gasp claws up my throat and escapes my lips.

If Marcie was bad, then Frank is so much worse.

My eyes take in the scene in pieces. His head pressed against the fryer, face burned and blackened; melted where it's touching the burners. The sight makes my stomach churn, and I clap a hand over my mouth to stop from throwing up all over the crime scene.

He's still holding a knife in his hand, like he was trying to avenge his wife or, more likely, save himself. In death it's clutched in his bony, too-long fingers that rest by the sink. Slashes mark his arm, the same kind that had cut through Marcie's body in so many places.

I'm sure they aren't from a knife, but I'm not in a position to do some kind of analysis on the weapon used to kill the Owens couple.

But it isn't just his face that makes me want to shrivel up on the diner kitchen floor. It's the rest of him. The arm wrenched out of its socket; the skin flayed open so I can see muscle underneath. He died more violently than his wife, and a small voice in the back of my head says that he deserved to.

He was just as bad as Billy Owens, after all.

I edge past him and try to look everywhere but at his seared off face. It's the worst part of the whole picture, though the muscles I can see in his arm and shoulder make my stomach churn as well. I could leave, I reason, as I stare at the floor instead of at him. I *should* leave.

But I have to know what's behind door number three.

Eyes fixed on the dragging blood stain that adorns the linoleum at my feet, I follow it with my eyes up to the door that leads to the back office. It's ajar, standing open enough that I don't need to go much further to see what's inside.

Besides, I already know, don't I?

It's Billy.

Billy Owens, who had been the bane of my existence, is sprawled on the desk with fewer wounds than the others, like he was granted some kind of mercy that his parents provided. Even in death he looks like an asshole, and my eyes linger on the jagged cuts adorning his hands and arms, the black eye. My body takes that moment to tell me that my time is up.

I can't do this anymore.

My head reels and I turn on my heel, nearly slipping in the same place as before as I run past Frank's body, then skirt past Marcie's as I arrive back in the front of the fifties diner.

Does it smell like death, or is it just me?

The diner looks different from this angle, though it might be my tunneling-vision as I stumble and trip around the metal bar. A jingle in my ears, like bells hitting on the glass door, registers in my head as I stare at the wavering, pulsing floor and try my damndest to make it back to the front before I collapse.

I don't make it.

My feet give out and I fall, only to be caught by hands around my shoulders that drag me back to my feet so I can meet disapproving brown eyes set in a lean, handsome face.

"You shouldn't be here," my therapist, Gabriel Brooks, admonishes gently. "What are you doing, Quinn? Didn't I tell you to be a good girl and let me take care of this?"

"You killed them," I whisper, finally noticing the blood on his face and his white tee that stands out sharply against the rest of him. "You *killed* them," I say again, making the words more real.

He tilts his head to the side, studying my face. "I killed them," he agrees. "Because he hurt you. Why would I ever let that go?"

"Because—I didn't ask you to—you can't *kill people* like this! You *slaughtered* them." My voice fades to a whisper, heart pounding rabbit-fast in my chest as my entire being looks for a way to escape.

He could kill me too, with whatever weapon he used on the Owens family. He could shred me into a million pieces, while I just watch.

"They deserved it,." He shrugs, hand coming up to my face again so he can cradle my cheek against his palm. "Sweet girl, they deserved every bit for what he did. I took care of it for you. I took care to make sure no one will ever stop to question that you'd done anything wrong."

"How could you do this?" I whisper, my hands trembling where they're pressed to his shoulders. "How could you—"

"The same way I've done it every single time before, of course."

The horrified shock on my face elicits delightful surprise on his, and his eyes glitter. "Oh no, oh *Quinn*, did you really think this was my first time? Darling, no. I was getting a little restless, actually. You gave me the perfect opportunity to let off some steam. I should thank you—"

"Don't say that!" I rip myself free of him, stumbling into the bar and nearly falling. His face falls in concern, but when he steps toward me, I grope around the bar for a weapon, finally holding a large piece of shattered glass between us. "Move," I tell him, trying to ignore the way my hand shakes.

5

Gabriel doesn't. He combs his fingers through his messy, light brown hair and tilts his head to the side to watch me like I'm a particularly interesting animal. "You'll hurt yourself," he informs me, glancing down at the glass. "You could never hurt me."

"I'll give it the best I've got," I threaten. "If you don't *move*."

He holds my stare for a few more agonizing seconds, deliberation plain on his face before he shrugs. "All right," he says at last. "But I'll find you later, when all of this has blown over. You won't tell, Quinn. We both know that, and I'll certainly be fine."

He moves to the side, waving his arms with a flourish like he's inviting me to leave. I pause, my fingers so tight on the glass that it cuts into my skin, and dart forward toward the door.

Before I reach it, one hand closes around my shoulder, the other gripping my wrist so I can't use the glass against him. "But don't go far, all right? We're not done, Quinn. Not by a longshot."

"Yes we are," I hiss, yanking away from him. He lets me go and I take off without another look or word, slamming open the diner door as he leans against the counter and watches me go like he doesn't hear the sirens in the distance or see the blood spattered on the wall beside him.

He may not get caught, but I'll take whatever time I have to run as far as I can, to make sure he never finds me as long as he's alive.

TWO

While I'm not exactly a snob, I can't bring myself to enjoy Akron's pizza. Maybe it's the fact that a lot of it borders on Chicago style, which to me is barely pizza, or that I just don't like most tomato sauces. Either way, when I look down at the slice in my hand that was given out free by our campus's student union, I let out a breath of disappointment through my nose.

But hey, free is free. Especially to a foster-turned-scholarship kid with a freshly minted social work degree and nothing to use it on. Yet, anyway. Because there's definitely work for me in Akron, if I really want it.

Preferably, though, I want to work somewhere else. Somewhere out of Ohio, and further than the few hundred miles that separate me from Springwood, where I grew up.

You're being dumb, I tell myself, choking down a bite of pizza like it's made of cardboard or slime. Then again, this pizza is congealed and cheap enough that I probably would have preferred slime-covered cardboard to some extent. *It's been five years, and he's over a hundred miles away.* Not quite two hundred, if I'm being exact, but one hundred and ninety-three-point-four miles is enough for me to call it *hundreds*.

And it isn't just that. There's no way Gabriel Brooks could show his face anywhere after the investigation.

Hell, I'm not even sure if he's still alive.

My chest twists at the flashbacks that try to overwhelm me, and I gnaw on shitty pizza in an attempt to make them go away as I walk. With all of my stuff already packed up to leave, the problem now really is figuring out where to actually *go*. I could live out of my car if I have to. I have before, and I have to be gone in two days from my dorm, or risk getting forcibly evicted. There's probably not a good chance that they'd let me stay as the janitor or wayward RA who's already graduated.

But the job in New York had said I might not hear from them until Monday, and that leaves me forty-eight hours of homelessness, joblessness, and wondering what I'll do. My stomach tries to twist at that as well, but I quell it with pizza as I walk on the sidewalk that will take me out of campus and toward a few cheap restaurants that have become favorites of mine over the years.

If I'm lucky, the Oregon job will get back to me before then. Today, maybe. Tomorrow at the latest. But God, I want to go to New York. I want to go somewhere new, and Oregon isn't the idea that tickles my brain just now. Maybe later, when I can leave my junior social worker job and apply for something better, I'll go across the states to LA or the desert.

But for now, it puts me at odds with myself. It's not that I'm afraid.

I'm usually only afraid of things that are trying to kill me or force their way into my room on a dark and stormy night.

But I'm... unsure.

Absently, I dodge around a couple of other students, wishing the weather was warmer. Not that it mattered to me like it did everyone else when the rain had threatened our graduation. There was no one there to take my picture or make memories with me.

There never had been.

My steps continue on the sidewalk as I swallow the last bite of lumpy pizza. It's good enough to last me until dinner, but I've decided that since I've graduated with all honors, a milkshake everyday this weekend is in order. It certainly helps that one of my cheap hideaways is having a special on them all weekend, so I don't have to do more than scrape a few quarters together in order to actually feed my lactose addiction.

It isn't long before I reach the small diner, and I walk in as thoughts of another diner from years ago try to press into my brain from all sides. Sometimes the memories are worse than others, but today isn't so bad. The seventies decor doesn't make me stop and stare, and it takes only a nudge to get my thoughts under control as I step up to the counter and smile at the older woman with curly gray hair cascading to her butt.

"Good morning, Quinn," she greets in a high, scratchy voice. It's somewhere between vocal fry, smoker's lungs, and excitement, but I've certainly never thought to ask. "How was graduation?"

Her question catches me off guard, and I look at her for a moment before replying. "It was good. It was *cold*," I amend, sharing a smile with her. "A lot of people were pissed their pictures were ruined by the weather, but I'm sure they'll get over it."

At least they have pictures.

I force the unexpected thought away, not liking the jealousy bubbling up in my insides. It's never a good look for anyone, especially me. "Can I get a medium mint milkshake, please?" I produce five quarters from my jacket, but she shakes her head and waves for me to put them back in my pocket.

"We'll make it a large, and it's on the house since you just graduated. Are you going to any good parties? Have any plans on where you'll go next?"

Not a one.

I don't say that either, but I do shake my head. "Thank you. I really appreciate you guys, and I don't know what I'll do without your milkshakes. I'm just waiting to hear back about a couple job offers, actually, but I'm probably moving to New York." The optimism hides the nerves that flicker in my voice, and she doesn't notice.

Instead, she talks about normal things, being friendly and polite until she slides my milkshake back across the counter. I tell her goodbye, accepting her well wishes, and leave before the smile slides right off my face and to the ground below.

Must be nice, I think, to assume everyone else has the same shit in life you do. Good for her. Good for them, I guess.

Still, the milkshake is better than normal, and I hum softly in surprise as I turn down the street toward the end of the block. The quickest way back to my dorm isn't back through campus, and since I hate walking, exercise, and sweating, I'm always looking for shortcuts. Especially on days like today when the foot traffic in Akron is noticeably more than normal, like everyone is parading about to celebrate the end of a week of bad weather.

I don't take my eyes off the prize as I walk. One foot in front of the other, I make my way to the end of the block, wait, and cross. Then I do it again, the timer in my head counting down at stop lights until I can move.

Wait and cross. Just wait and cross on repeat, and within a few blocks, I've made it to the backside of campus, where the dorms tower above the rest of the university. Not that it's much of a contest, when the academic buildings are, at most, three stories tall and the highest dorm, Fernwood, is eight.

It's huge, has a lot of rooms, and as it's the building they stuff all the freshmen, the rest of us stay clear of it as much as we can. Our university is hard to get into and harder to stay in, so about twenty percent of those freshmen won't make it to the next year. If they do, they'll be much less irritating, at least.

I'm just about to cross back into campus when a hand grabs me, and my stomach plummets as I'm towed backward to the front of the shop behind me. My hand tightens on my mint shake like a lifeline, and my hand comes up to grab the man's wrist as he stares down at me with suspicious, worried eyes.

He's gorgeous, my brain says, taking the worst time in the world to note the man's soft-looking black hair and full mouth. His eyes are a darker brown than what I prefer, or what I was expecting, and there's a light sheen of sweat on his forehead as he looks at me.

"Let go," I tell him quietly, noting that we're in an empty enough area that no one is stopping to see if something's wrong. "Let go, or I'll scream."

"Don't scream," the man murmurs, loosening his grip on my arm. "I just want to help you."

My eyebrows jerk upward, and I can't help the unimpressed, disbelieving frown that pulls at my lips. "No *offense*, friend, but men who grab me and shove me against a wall aren't my idea of help. What do you want?" I don't want to throw my milkshake at him, but I will if I need to so I can get away.

Still, even though I know he could hurt me, he doesn't *scare* me. My heart doesn't race. My blood doesn't cool in my veins. I haven't been afraid of anyone in over four years, and he's not what'll do it now.

Even if he stabs me and I bleed out on the ground, I don't know if I'll taste the same fear as I had before.

"He's looking for you." The words drag my attention out of that abyss inside of me that's gotten bigger and bigger over the years. His voice is rushed and soft, and he changes positions so this doesn't look so non-consensual. "I didn't know it was you until today, and it's hard to warn you when he's watching."

My heart skips a beat, but I refuse to think the worst. "Who?" I ask, taking my time to ask the question. "Who do you think is following me? And who the hell are you?"

"My name is Wren." He pulls his hands away and lifts them up in surrender. "I don't normally help people, but..." He shakes his head as he trails off. "I've seen what he'll do. If he's following you, it's to do more than just hurt you. You need to run."

"Who's following me?" I demand, my bravado falling from my tone. I don't know this man, this *Wren*, any more than I know the people walking by. He doesn't know me, and he's probably some drunken, drugged up tweaker.

I don't need to listen to him.

"Look, dude—"

"You ever met a guy named Gabriel Brooks?"

Time stops, and my world shatters. I feel it and hear it break into pieces around me, and for a long moment I wonder if I'll fall, or if my legs will simply give out so I can fall through the ground.

My lips tingle, numb, and the shake falls from limp fingers to splatter all over our shoes below us. "No," I say, refusing to hear him. "No."

With racing thoughts, I look away, to either side, like Gabriel is standing there, waiting to make an entrance. Suddenly every stranger could be him, and every hood hides his face while my heart slams into my ribs to try to make some grand escape.

"No," I say again, looking back up at Wren. "You're wrong—"

"*Run*," he tells me, stepping back. "If you're what he's after, if you've done something to him? *Run*. And never stop running for anything. Do you understand me?"

Of course I understand; I understand better than he can ever know. Even as nausea claws at my stomach and my soul tries to abandon the rest of me, I prepare to do exactly what he's told me to.

Run.

THREE

I don't think I've ever run so fast in my life.

The fact that I nearly get hit by a car does little to penetrate my panic, and I only run faster to hit the sidewalk on the other side. Thankfully, I was already close and know the route by heart; my sprint takes me down a winding path through the back of campus that I half-ignore, choosing instead to trample on the landscaping beside it in my mad dash.

By the time I'm back at the dorm and my heart is threatening to quit, I'm gasping for air and clutching my side. Cramps are real, and my lungs burn while I stumble through the glass doors of my dormitory. It's warm enough that I'm sweating, and I slam the elevator button hard enough that I'm surprised it doesn't break.

"Quinn?" The voice behind me belongs to my RA, and I turn with a pained smile on my face to see her. "Are you okay?" she asks, concern lining her face and entwined in her words. "You look…" She doesn't say terrible, but I have a feeling she wants to.

"Totally fine," I tell her, still breathing hard with my hands on my sides like I'm trying to hold myself together. "Great. Wonderful. I just need to get back to my laptop for a job email. You get it." I don't know if she gets it, or if I'm making sense at all, but I need her to back the fuck up so I can pant in peace.

"Yeah," she agrees, giving me a supportive smile. "We're having a pizza party in the theater tonight, by the way. You coming?"

No. I'm not. I'll be busy running away, being anywhere but here. But I make a show of thinking about it, then nod like I'll consider the invitation.

"Maybe, if this call goes well." The elevator dings and I cross my fingers, only belatedly realizing I'd told her email, or something.

But who gives a fuck?

Mashing the elevator button for the doors to close, I give her a false, wide smile and pray for the elevator to *move*. When the doors finally do close, I fall back against the metal of the back wall, groaning.

Where could he be?

Akron, obviously. But how has he been following me? I don't do much except go to class, get milkshakes, study, and sometimes fall asleep in the library. Though, the thought of him watching me while I snore and drool on my textbooks on the third floor makes me shudder.

How did he find me?

That's the real question. I'd wanted to go further. I'd hoped to go further, actually. But after a year, my really good scholarship had been cut off, and I'd had to come back from Nevada to go to school in Akron. But even then, it had been a year and a half since I'd heard from him, and from my information, he'd fled from Springwood with the police on his heels.

So why doesn't he have better things to do than be *here*, stalking me?!

My door protests when I slam the key into the lock, and ricochets off the wall at the force I open it. My roommate is gone, having packed up before graduation and leaving the moment it was over. She'd been nice, but not nice enough for us to really be friends. While I don't think she hated me, I'm glad now that she hadn't tried to stick around or needed to stay for a few extra days, like I did.

Though, that plan is out the window and shot dead. Very dead.

With my heart still pounding in my ears and my vision still questionable, I look around and momentarily freeze, my hands still working to pull my shoulder-blade length black hair into a ponytail.

What am I doing?

I want to pack. I need to pack, obviously, like I have every time I've needed to escape or go somewhere new.

But now, surrounded by the mess of the few things that I've kept for myself and made mine, I don't know what to do. The smartest thing to do would be to leave it, but rationality kicks me in the ears as I consider that option. Without any of my stuff, or my money, or my computer, I won't be able to do anything at all. I need my things, and it isn't like I have a lot.

Will thirty minutes or so really kill me?

God, I hope not.

Sucking in a breath, I try to channel my inner foster child. I don't go for the garbage bags, because something tender and fragile in me will break if I do, but I haul out my two duffel bags and get to work throwing my clothes into one of them, followed by my shoes. Personal things go next, and I've zipped that one up and half the second one half full when I realize, with a jolt of relief, I'm basically done.

Sure, it's tragic as fuck that I don't even have enough to my name to fill a dorm room, but in this situation, it's helpful. It's necessary, even, and when I stare at the white-washed walls and empty room, I can't help the sadness raking at me.

I can't help the way I pause, or the way my feet want to drag so I can look at this place for just a while longer. My home for three years hasn't been much, but it has been the safest place I've ever had. Even before Gabriel, I hadn't known safety in Springwood. I hadn't known what it was like to look around and have things that really, actually belonged to me.

I'd just felt... lost.

Closing my eyes hard, I suck in a breath, let it out, then repeat the process. Out of every moment in time to fall apart, this has to be the absolute worst one. I need to leave. Now that I'm packed and I have nothing left to do or get, I need to go. Emails, calls, texts... they can all wait until I'm in my car and out of Akron.

Surely if I'm fast enough, Gabriel Brooks will think I'm still here. Or at least, he won't know where to look for me. Glancing toward the door, I frown at the pink mug on my roommate's desk. I'd told her she'd left it here, but Kaye had just snorted and told me to chuck it for her, or let maintenance do it. I still haven't, and at this point I'm not making a trip to the trash can. The condition of our room is what it is. Things will be fine, or at least as fine as they can be.

"Okay..." I murmur, glancing around one more time to make sure I hadn't forgotten anything. "I think you're good to go, Quinn. Now it's time to actually do the thing." I walk forward, hand on the doorknob, and give the room one last, last look.

I have everything I need for an escape, and once the door is open and braced, I'll drag my bags to the elevator and down to the parking lot.

"You look like you're all ready to go somewhere." The cool, neutral voice hits me hard, my fingers slipping from the door, even though I refuse to look back at the frame.

"Not Nevada though, right? I didn't think the desert agreed with you, though you did get such a nice tan there."

How does he know? The words whisper through my brain and every fear, every bit of anxiety I've ever felt floods my body tenfold.

I'm not afraid of anything.

Except for him.

"I bet you burned," I say flatly, turning my gaze on the man leaning against the doorframe. "You're too pale for that much sun." It isn't quite true, though his complexion is a few shades lighter than mine.

A smile flicks across his lips, warm hazelnut eyes dancing as he lifts his hand that holds the same kind of cup my shake had been in. "I don't get your fascination with *mint*. Don't you taste it enough when you brush your teeth?" I can't tear my eyes away from his as he sucks on the straw, gaze never leaving mine. "The lady at the counter was so nice, though. They think a lot of you, there."

"Go away," I say, the words a whispered plea, and not the command I want them to be.

"But I just got here," Gabriel replies, eyes wide and earnest. It's not real, though. Nothing about this act is real. He reaches up with his free hand to comb his fingers through light brown hair that's a little longer than I remember, and when I blink, I realize he looks older.

But I suppose I do too.

It's been five years, and Gabriel looks worn out. There's impatience and frustration in the lines of his face now, and while he barely looked thirty back when we both lived in

Springwood, he now looks every bit of thirty-five. Unfortunately, it's not a bad look on him.

"I don't want you here," I say, hating that I back up when he takes a step forward. "I don't want you to be here, Gabriel."

"I figured, based on the frantic packing," Gabriel admits, eyeing up my duffel bags. "But why is that, exactly? What have I ever done to hurt you, Quinn? What have I ever said to make you think I was a danger to you?" He pushes into the room and closes the door behind him, causing my heart to sink so low I worry it'll burn up in my currently rolling stomach.

"You killed them," I remind him, my hands curled into fists. "You *slaughtered* the Owens. I saw it. I saw what you did to him, his face, his—"

"Well, maybe they shouldn't have raised such a shitty son, hmm? Maybe they shouldn't have been complicit, or wanted to go to the cops about you." His words are matter-of-fact, like he doesn't care at all about what I've just said. "But I don't think I've ever heard you say thank you."

"Because I haven't. And I don't intend to," I say, trying to steel my nerves and lend some of that to my voice. "Because I didn't do anything wrong back then. I was a kid who fucked up, because of something that happened that was out of her control. So I went to you for *help*, and you made everything worse." My nails cut into my palms, though I barely notice the sharp pain. I'm much too fixated on him, and the way he sets the milkshake on my desk ever so gently.

"That's not how I remember it," he says, and his slow, careful movements vanish as he strides across the room. I stumble backward, surprised, and my legs hit my roommate's bed beside her desk, giving Gabriel the perfect opening to lunge forward and grab my chin in his hand, body trapping me in place as he towers over me. "And I worry that you're lying to yourself, Quinn. Maybe you should schedule another session with your therapist." His nails dig lightly into my jaw as he stares at me, face calculating.

"My therapist sucked and didn't understand my needs," I hiss, eyes darting around the room. "What do you want? An apology? A *thank you*?" I find I don't want to give him either, and the thought of doing so makes my lips burn. "Tell me how to make you leave."

"I want you," Gabriel replies, his tone level.

It's so easy, so honest, that I stop looking for an escape from the empty room. I stare up at him, confused and terrified, and find frightening honesty in that gorgeous face. "No, you don't," I say, mostly because I refuse to believe it's true. "No, you fucking don't, you psycho—"

"I'm willing to forgive a lot of this, as I know you're scared," he interrupts, though he doesn't sound particularly impressed. "But I'm only so patient. I told you back then that I'd be back for you. I just hadn't expected it to be this long of a wait for either of us."

"Sorry, but I'm not looking for a travel buddy," I reply, seeing the pink mug out of the corner of my eye. I try not to draw attention to it, though, and instead keep my attention steadily fixed on him. "I don't even think you'll have enough room in my car."

"No, that's not what I was saying, baby girl," Gabriel admits, a smile pulling at his lips. It's not nice, not like the smiles he gave me when I was his patient. It's cruel, and wanting.

It's psychotic. Just like he is.

"I'm saying that you and I are going *home*. In case you haven't been up to date on Springwood news, I've been cleared of any wrongdoing. I was even given an apology. Everything is oh so wonderful there now, except for one tiny problem. Do you want to guess what that is?"

"People still know you're crazy?" I assume, thoughts flying at the speed of light. "You still can't sleep?"

"You're not there like you're supposed to be." He jerks me to my feet, a gasp leaving me as I stumble into his solid warmth.

"I'm not coming home with you," I tell him, heart pounding with panic. "I won't go *anywhere* with you. Not *ever*."

"Never is a long time," he points out, grin wide and cold. "And I have a lot of ways to make you see things my way."

"I'll kill you," I tell him, the words escaping my lips before I can stop to think about them. "I'll kill you, I'll *hurt* you. Because I'm not afraid of you, and I'm not going with you. Not now, not ever, *never*." I spit the words at him, but he shrugs and takes a step toward the door, not realizing that he's putting me closer to my goal. He's helping me, but I can't let him know. Not when he yanks again and I stagger more than I probably need to, putting me in range of the mug on the desk.

"I don't really believe you," he admits, hand tight on my upper arm. "But I'm really looking forward to you surprising me, Quinn. Once we're home."

"Then believe this, *Doctor*." I don't know where I get the strength, though I assume it has to be from desperation. All I know is that I grab the mug handle and whirl around, the ceramic *cracking* against his skull and causing Gabriel to crumple to the ground in a dead faint.

FOUR

E ven though I'm reasonably sure he'll be out for at least a few minutes, I'm still terrified that he's going to appear in the parking lot behind me as I throw my suitcases into my trunk, probably with a knife to end my life then and there.

But he's never tried to hurt you, a very unhelpful part of my brain reminds me coolly, as if it has any right to do so.

"Shut up," I whisper to myself, throwing myself into the driver's seat of my '05 Camry that's starting to fall apart. All I need is for it to get me somewhere that's not here. Then it can die or combust, for all I care.

As long as it does so outside of Akron.

"You're fine," I tell myself, pulling out into traffic. There's steel in my voice that I force into existence, and coolness floods my veins as I create distance between myself and Gabriel. In hindsight, I should've called the police.

But the thought twists my stomach unpleasantly, and instead of trying to examine the root of the feeling, I shake it off and throw it in the trunk with my stuff. I won't call the cops, because I don't have time and I don't want to deal with the questions. Not because Gabriel Brooks is undeserving of jail time. Hands tightening on the steering wheel, I work to calm myself down the rest of the way by working through my thoughts in sections.

He won't know where I've gone.

He has no way of following me.

I have no reason to fear Gabriel.

The last part isn't precisely true, and my brain reminds me of that by walking through a mental picture of the Owens' diner without my consent. I remember the way Marcie looked so limp, like a rag doll.

I remember the smell that had invaded my nostrils when I'd walked past her husband, and the way his face had melted onto the grill, with—

A car honks and I jerk back into my lane, cursing myself and my wandering attention. I can't do this right now. I don't have the time or the freedom to fall apart, and I wonder if I've gone soft in the years since escaping my final foster home.

I used to be so good at compartmentalizing. At making things seem less real than they actually are. But without having to do it in a long time, I'm finding that it's harder than it ever was before.

You're escaping into your daydreams. Dr. Brooks' voice echoes in my head and this time I don't put the brakes on the memory, since it isn't accompanied by the smell of burned flesh and too much blood. *Do you find yourself needing them to get through the day, Quinn?*

He'd sat in front of me, on a sofa draped with a black, soft blanket, while I'd stuffed myself into an armchair. His office had always been so friendly, so welcoming, that I'd wondered if he'd decorated it or had his secretary do it instead. The pillows had been the expensive kind, not cheap and rough fabric. I should know, since I spent so much time running my hands over their seams as if looking for a way to take out their insides.

I need them, I'd admitted, half to him and half to myself. *But you don't understand, Dr. Brooks. It isn't because I like to daydream or make up stories in my head.*

I'd seen it then. His face had fallen slightly, and he'd clutched the pen in his hand just a little tighter. *You need them because they hurt you.*

I manage to slam to a stop in front of a red light, mouth set in a line as I'm nearly thrown through my windshield. I need to calm down and chill the fuck out. Otherwise, I'm accidentally going to off myself before I even get out of Akron.

My phone rings as the light turns green, making me jump, and I reach out blindly to curl my fingers around it before setting it to speaker and answering the call from a number I don't know. "Hello?" I ask, voice politely bemused. If this is a job offer, I don't need to sound hysterical out of the gate.

"*Miss Riley?*" The woman on the other end sounds as polite as I do, and I imagine that she's putting on an act, same as me.

"This is her. Can I help you?" God, this had better be an agency I'd interviewed with.

"*My name is Melinda Yates. We spoke the other day?*" Realization slams into me, and I remember the sweet-faced, older lady who had interviewed me from an agency in Kentucky. *Rural* Kentucky, I'd realized, when I'd looked it up after the meeting. It's not my first choice of jobs, but if she's offering me one, then I'm a little nervous at the prospect of turning it down.

"Oh, hi!" I say, like the realization brings me joy. "It's so good to hear from you." She'd been a backup interview, with a place I hadn't really wanted to work but felt like I had to apply to, due to my worries about getting into a social work career anywhere big, like New York. My demands for Kentucky had been too high, I know. It had been my way of turning them off of hiring me, and I'm surprised she's called me just to tell me that.

"*We've been discussing what you asked for in terms of salary.*" Here it comes. The denial I expect and am half hoping for. "*And we're willing to meet your asking wage.*"

What?

"*If you're still interested in the job, we'd love to have you start on Tuesday. Would that be possible?*"

I don't know what to say. Or even know how to feel, since this is equal parts fortunate and unfortunate. I want to tell her no, that I'm waiting for a call from somewhere else instead. I want to tell her that there's no way in hell I'm dragging my ass down to *Kentucky* to work, especially some western lake-town near a prison that seems like the last stop before hell.

"That would be perfect," I find myself saying instead as logic takes over. I've known the other jobs are a longshot, and there's probably nothing saying I can't last minute decline this job before taking one of those. At least, I hope so.

And this gives me somewhere to go. Plus, the cost of living there seems to be dirt-cheap, meaning that I wouldn't have to live in a cardboard box. Gabriel, from what he knows of me, would never suspect me to go to Kentucky. Especially since I'd shared with him my dreams of moving to a bigger city.

It's perfect, in the worst possible way.

"Thank you so much, Mrs. Yates. I'm really excited to start on Tuesday." Excitement isn't the word that rings true in my head, but I want to sound as enthusiastic and bright-eyed as possible so she doesn't dislike me without meeting me first. "Will you send me the information through email, please? I've actually just left my college, so I'll head that way now. And starting on Tuesday gives me time to find a place to rent, even short-term." I'll probably have to find a hotel for a couple of days, or a cheap backyard cabin that was once owned by serial killing moonshiners. That seems more in my price range.

"*No problem, Quinn. My sister rents out some homes in the area, if you'd like to check them out? I could send you her number?*"

The homes had better be cheap, but I don't say that. "I would be really grateful." If they are, or they're apartments, then maybe I could get everything taken care of today. That would be nice and give me a chance to sleep off the panic draining out of my veins. "Just send me everything and I'll be there bright and early on Tuesday. Thank you so much, again."

"*You're actually working a bit of a later shift,*" the social worker informs me sweetly. "*I hope that's alright?*"

Great. Graveyard shift; here I come. But as beggars can't be choosers, I tell her that I am just so perfectly happy with that arrangement and say goodbye.

Maybe it's a blessing. Probably not, since I don't believe in those, but I *am* a night person, after all. If my shift is as late as I'm afraid it is, at least I'll be more awake for it, hopefully.

Then again, as long as Gabriel Brooks isn't there, I'm sure I'll be able to manage.

THE BEST THING that can be said about the house at 402 Knickview Road in Eddyville, Kentucky, is that it isn't nearly as bad as I'd expected it to be. It isn't a cardboard box, there's electricity, internet, and even running water.

Which, being from a small town in Ohio and ending up in homes that sometimes didn't have hot water or working, reliable internet, is still enough of a selling point for me to agree to the price and immediately drag my stuff in from the car.

Marian Yates, who reminds me quite a bit of her sister and my new boss, watches me with abject horror in her eyes when it's clear that I have literally nothing else to my name. "You're okay, right honey?" she asks, with all the motherly worry that she can muster.

Though I smile, the look is probably too wide and too happy for the occasion. "I am," I promise. "I'm totally okay. It's just that I don't have a lot."

"It's furnished," she says, like I hadn't just done a walk-through of the two bed, two two bath home that's somewhere just under fifteen-hundred square feet. "And if you need anything else, I'm sure we can get it for you."

I need to sleep. The seven and a half hour drive meant that it's almost dark now that I'm ready to go into the house and pass out, and part of me wishes I'd broken it up into two days. The other, more rational part of me is thrilled I hadn't, since now I have two whole days to sleep and eat junk food before I start my first shift as a social worker.

Which is a worry I'll save for some time other than *now*.

"It's really okay," I assure her, and lift my bag of gas station groceries to show her that I won't starve, either. "I'm pretty happy to be able to call it home. It's really great, Mrs. Yates, thank you."

She waves a hand at me. "You don't have to be so formal with me, honey. Just Marian will do. And if you need anything at all, my husband and I live just over there." She points at a considerably cleaner, better lit house down the road. "You let me know, and we'll be out here in a minute or two. Okay?"

"I will." I doubt I'll ever actually do it, but I smile at the offer with as much appreciation as I can muster in my tired brain. "Thank you again for this. I really appreciate it." I'd like it more if she left me alone so I could pass out for a while.

"Anytime. Have a good night, Quinn. And welcome to Eddyville." She says it like there's something here to be proud of. Like it isn't some small town at the edge of a few lakes in western Kentucky.

The only thing that it has going for it, in my mind, is the lack of serial killing therapists, though I suppose that could change if I'm incredibly unlucky.

How would he know? I ask myself cynically, my thoughts dripping with disbelief as I drag myself up the rickety deck and into the house. It smells clean, at least. Like Marian had sprayed Lysol in here when she'd known I was coming. That's fine with me, though. More than fine, since there's nothing questionable, dirty, or dangerous as far as my eyes can tell.

There were a lot worse places to end up. And moving in has gotten my mind off of the email from the agency in New York that I'd seen when I'd checked for the information Melinda had sent. As I'd hoped against, they'd politely declined hiring me, telling me they would consider me in the future.

Not that I believe a form letter.

"It could be worse," I tell myself, dropping onto the sofa and pressing the power button on the remote until the television flickers on. The living room is small, with just enough space for a couch, coffee table, and tv in an old-fashioned entertainment center perched against the opposite wall. There are wear marks on the wooden floor, and the couch feels like it's played host to dozens of behinds over the years before I'd had the nerve to sit on it.

"Things could *always* be worse."

FIVE

T hings don't get worse for the entire weekend. No matter how many times I stalk to the window and stare out of it like I'm in a bad horror movie and waiting for the inevitable monster to creep up my driveway, it never happens.

Gabriel never shows up, and every time I stare out a window picked at random, I feel dumber than the last time I'd done it.

Kentucky is far away from anywhere I've even thought about going. There's no reason for him to look for me here, or even come here, truth be told. The whole place feels a little too rural for him, and I doubt the perfect Dr. Gabriel Brooks even likes lake country.

Hell, I'm not even sure I do. I've played with the idea of renting a boat with money I don't have and discovering the art of fishing, which I don't think I'd be very good at. Would it be hot? Would I have to get up early in the mornings like I've seen on the nature documentaries I keep finding on my newly acquired cable?

I don't realize I'm glaring until I meet the eyes of one of my neighbors as he walks his dog down to the end of the street. The balding, blond man gives me an uneasy look and turns, like *I'm* the monster in the movie, and not the inevitable final girl.

"Great," I mutter to myself, and walk back to the small, cluttered kitchen to dump the remains of my coffee. While my shift isn't exactly graveyard, it isn't the normal nine to five, either. I'm supposed to be at the office at noon, and I won't be done until eight. Not awful, but not exactly my idea of a good time. Not to mention, I'm currently on a trial, probationary run. I work for four days a week, instead of five, and naturally I don't have health insurance. God bless America.

But as long as I don't get stabbed or pneumonia from my constant lurking at windows, I doubt I'll have much need for it. Back when I'd been under eighteen, the state had paid for my healthcare, and my therapy. When I'd lost that, Dr. Brooks had oh-so-helpfully taken me as a pro bono patient.

What a nice fucking guy.

I shove the thought of him from my head, hating that he exists there without me wanting him to. It seems nearly impossible to stop thinking about him, and the worst part is...

Not all the thoughts are bad ones.

But the ones that aren't are a little easier to push away for now, especially when I set my mind to tasks like grabbing my keys, doing one last check to ensure my flat iron won't burn the house down into ashes. Then I lock the door behind me on my way to my old car that somehow hasn't exploded.

It's good for me that it hasn't, since I still need it to get to and from work. My newly rented house is too far away from the Eddyville office on the western side of town to be closer to its neighbor, Kuttawa, for me to walk to. Until I can afford the payments on something newer, prayer and duct tape had better keep this one running.

The drive is easy, if a little boring. Eddyville is even more rural than Springwood was, and the only interesting parts of it are when I get to look at the lake and see people speeding along in fishing boats or larger pontoons.

After twenty minutes of weaving in and out of the country traffic and wondering if I need more coffee, I pull into the Social Services Office of Eddyville... and just look at it.

Holy shit, my brain provides, staring up at the tiny building no bigger than a café and much less interesting to look at. *This is so small.* The exterior is dark brick, with a cheery white door that plays host to laminated paper signs I can't read from here.

Even the property itself is small, with the nearest building being a McDonald's with much more traffic and curbside appeal than this. Slowly, I walk up the cement sidewalk, eyeing the cracks and chips missing from parts of it and providing evidence that this place is just as old as it looks. The land-scaping is tidy, with small flower beds bordering the sides of the small building and a white sign that identifies it as *Eddyville Social Services Office* stuck in the ground and painted with black, cracked letters.

It certainly isn't like the other places I'd applied to, that's for sure.

Without hesitating, I grab the doorknob, and only succeed in pulling instead of pushing, as the bright green, printed sign reminds me to do with a cheery smiley face. I roll my eyes and *push* instead, causing the door to swing forward on squeaky hinges.

The first face I see inside is one that reminds me enough of Marian's that this has to be my new boss, Melinda Yates. She beams from ear to ear, tortoiseshell glasses perched on the end of her nose and held there by two beaded chains that loop back around her neck. Her hair is more grey than blonde, and she's already too friendly, just by the look alone.

But I return the smile and walk inside, trying to remind myself not to ignore all the things she'll tell me about what I need to do in order to succeed in Eddyville.

Because, as I remind myself while she gives me a tour of the small office. I don't have anywhere else to succeed right now. It's here or nothing, and nothing isn't an option.

Especially when *nothing* sounds a lot like Springwood in my brain.

"Do you like to swim?" Melinda tries to get comfortable in her hard-backed chair as I watch, though it takes me a moment to drag my thoughts back to her question. It wasn't what I was expecting, since the Blaiken family are about to show up at any moment for their assessment with Melinda. It's a particularly sad case, by anyone's standards, and my heart thumps nervously in my chest at all the possible outcomes for two parents who had lost everything because of the dad's addiction to gambling.

They'd gone further and further down the rabbit hole until finally they couldn't afford to feed their kids and the dad was self-medicating with alcohol. According to Melinda, they're on the right track to getting their two daughters back, but the look on her face isn't exactly optimistic when she talks about them.

"Hmm?" I ask, needing a moment to actually hear her question and think it through.

"I was just wondering if you liked to swim. My husband and I host pool parties in the summer, and since it's getting unbearably warm, we're planning our first one. Marian told me you might enjoy some company and some time out. She says you haven't left the house much since you got here."

I hate pity. I hate her pity more since it's delivered with practiced kindness and sympathy.

Sympathy is almost as bad as pity.

"I've been tired," I say, cracking a smile. "And I do like to swim, though it's been awhile since I have." God, I wish the Blaikens would show up so I wouldn't have to do this right now. It's sad to think that their misery could save me from my own discomfort, and worse, that I'm begging for it. But what else will stop the words and kindness from pouring out of Melinda's mouth?

"You should come. I'll let you know the exact date when we figure it out. Probably next weekend, actually. Though there won't be too much swimming just yet. Water's still figuring out it's summer." She chuckles as the door opens, and from her office I see two adults walk in, both of them looking like they might be marching to their death.

As if sensing my discomfort, Melinda reaches out to pet my hand, though I wish she wouldn't. My fingers tense under her touch, and she gives me a comforting smile to go along with the unwanted touch. I don't know her. I don't want her hand on mine, even though she seems like an okay person.

But that isn't the point.

"It'll be fine," she promises, and opens the folder on her desk as one of the other social workers, Abby, directs the Blaikens toward her office. A bright, barely believable smile settles itself on Melinda's lips, and I try to give a less-than-morbid look to my own expression as the Blaikens walk in and sit on rickety, metal chairs that squeak and protest when they perch on them.

For a few moments while Melinda shuffles papers, the only sound in the room is the spinning fan on its stand in the corner. It rocks a little as it turns, giving it a noticeable squeak when it gets too far to one side. The *swish-swish* is predictable, and I find myself counting the swivels as Melinda leafs through the papers and I survey Mr. and Mrs. Blaiken.

They aren't what I expected. They don't beg or threaten. They don't look disinterested or even really poverty-stricken. In fact, they look... *normal.*

Like two, normal, down on their luck, humans who have made one too many mistakes in their lives. My heart clenches, twisting in my chest, and it's unfortunate that Mrs. Blaiken looks at me at the moment that I remember my mother's face, and how different it was from this woman's when I'd seen her last.

"She's new," Melinda murmurs, beaming as I try to fix my face. "I'm having her sit in with me so she can learn. Do either of you mind? She's very promising, and I'm hoping she can provide some insight on the help we can give you after today."

The last part of her sentence is what melts their apprehension, and Mrs. Blaiken turns on me again with wide, fearful eyes that try and fail to hide that she's terrified of Melinda right now. Or rather, what Melinda's judgment could mean for their family.

You should've left him, I say silently, glancing at her husband. He's better at hiding his feelings than his wife, but I can't help but remember the words I'd read in the file concerning them both. Their kids would be fine and living with them, if not for him and his problems.

Why didn't you leave him? I don't ask, because it isn't my place. It wasn't her fault initially, sure. But to just sit by and let her husband wreck her children's lives? It doesn't seem right to me, and something in me twists at the notion of her just *letting it happen.*

God, maybe my first sociology professor had been right when I'd opened up about my history of foster care. He told me that this job would most likely be harder for me than most, because my empathy would mean that I felt every case that was similar to my own more strongly than most.

I'd brushed him off then, but it hits me now that there's a good chance he was right.

Taking a deep breath, I force my body to relax. My fingers unclench, and my ribs pull away from the lungs they were trying to close in on. My heart stops pounding in my temples, and I look at them rationally, like I would a scenario back in school, instead of real life.

I can do this, and it's dumb of me to let my emotions get the best of me now, when I'm normally so good at keeping my feelings or sympathy at bay.

Melinda wastes no time in going over their reports with them, and from the beginning, I know it won't be good. There's a frown on her face that I haven't seen yet today, and she's careful to avoid words like *messed up* or *mistakes*. Even though I don't know how she skirts around them, since this whole ordeal is a clusterfuck.

Mr. Blaiken's drug test had come back positive. His wife had known, based on the disappointed acceptance on her face, and when she opens her mouth to speak, it isn't to condemn him or divorce him on the spot, like I'd hoped.

"What will happen to my kids?" she asks, her voice wobbling. "I know you said that he needed to pass this time, but..." She swallows hard. "Can we keep trying? He's trying so hard. It was just a mistake, and I know he can do better."

Melinda's face is sympathetic and kind, but not hopeful. "I'm afraid we're running out of options at this point, Mrs. Blaiken," she admits, looking from her to her husband with more understanding than I'd be able to muster. "I know we'd discussed your children coming home with you, but the first step is your husband's ability to not use or drink." She looks at him, still so understanding, and not at all like she wants to punch him.

But he won't look at her. He mutters a few words of explanation that I can barely hear, though none of them sound like the pleas and apologies he should be screaming out. If he cared about them, why not divorce her himself? He has to know that his wife would have a better chance of getting their kids back without him.

Unless he doesn't care.

By the time they leave, Mrs. Blaiken is crying. I watch her go, a handful of Melinda's pink-tinted tissues balled up in her hands, and force myself again to stop tensing every muscle in my body.

"It's hard," Melinda says, holding out the box of tissues. I shake my head and she puts them back, giving me a worried look.

"It's frustrating," I correct, waiting for the Blaikens to leave before I speak. "Why doesn't she just leave him? She has a job, and she's not the one drinking or using. She could get her kids back without him."

"I doubt that's even occurred to her," Melinda says, voice tinged with surprise at my words. "He's her husband. Her partner."

"He's the problem," I argue. "He's not a partner when he's the problem."

"You're very practical, though these situations rarely are." She closes the file and gets to her feet. I follow, rolling my shoulders, and she goes on, "Do you think you'd be able to leave the man you love, if you were in that situation?"

"Yes," I say without needing time to consider it. "The moment someone I love is hurting me is the moment I cut them off. You shouldn't let people have that much control over you."

Melinda looks me over, and for a few seconds I'm sure I've said something wrong and she's going to fire me on the spot. The fan *swish-swishes* behind me, and just before the inevitable squeak, Melinda smiles. "So practical," she chides, ushering me out of her office and toward the break room. "You'll have a hard time finding a husband with such radical views. And who knows? Maybe you're just young, and you'll probably feel differently once you're in love."

I don't agree. I couldn't disagree more, actually. But I just smile and give her a noncommittal answer of agreement. She's wrong, but then it doesn't matter. The only thing that matters is that I keep my job and make this work, at least until another, better option comes along.

CHAPTER

SIX

I t takes the phone ringing twice for me to remember that as the newest member of Eddyville Social Services, I have the shitty on call hours.

I sigh and open my eyes, staring at the ceiling of the small bedroom I'd claimed in Marian's house. I could let it just go to voicemail, but that's not part of my job. My hand darts out so I can grab my phone, and I answer it before it can go to voicemail and pull it to my face. "Hello?" I mumble, uncurling my legs and stretching them toward the bottom of the bed until my muscles protest.

"Did I wake you up?" Melinda's voice isn't tired, like she was up anyway, and I wonder if this is her normal social hour, or if there's a reason for her call. Right now, I can't decide which would be worse.

Of course she woke me up. But I swallow back the words and instead reply, "It's okay. What's up? Is something wrong?" Checking the digital clock beside the bed, I cringe. It's almost three in the morning. Prime sleeping time with my hours. But also, apparently, prime Melinda time.

"*I don't think so, but since you're the social worker on call tonight, I need you to check something out for me. It's more of a formality than anything, and a good way for you to get some experience doing this,*" my boss explains, her tone more cheerful than it has any right to be this late at night.

"You want me to go knock on someone's door at three am?" I ask, sitting up in bed and rubbing the heel of my palm against my eyes. I need to get my brain working properly if I'm going to go do what she's asking. Even though I don't want to.

"*Not exactly. They both normally check in with me by ten or so over email. They work late shifts and are a... bit of a special case. This has happened before, but I want a note to call me on their door by the time they wake up.*"

All I want to know is why a fucking email won't do.

Still, I suck in a breath and close my eyes hard, steeling myself for what I need to do. "All right," I say finally, getting to my feet. "Okay. Yeah, just text me the address? Is there a letter I should write or something?"

"*It's in the office's mailbox, if you're okay swinging by. It should be on your way.*" Clearly I'd underestimated how shitty of a boss Melinda can be when she wants to.

"Sure," I tell her, trying not to sigh sharply and make my disdain for the job super clear. "Shouldn't take me long, I hope." God, I hope it isn't that far. "I'll do all of that. And I'll let you know if I need anything or get lost." Without changing out of my pajama shorts, I drag on a pair of sweatpants and a light-weight hoodie.

"*That'll be fine. I'll be awake for a few more hours.*" At this point, she's just solidifying to me that she's some kind of ancient, eldritch demon that uses the night as her time to perform clandestine rituals, or something.

"Okay. I'll talk to you later." I manage to keep my neutral facade up until I hang up the phone and groan, wanting to flop right back down in bed and pretend that this entire thing was some lucid dream.

But I'm the one that wanted to do this. It's just my fault that I thought some rural lake town wouldn't demand hours like this.

WHILE I PROMISE myself that I won't judge, it's hard when the house comes into view.

Trash litters the yard, decorating the grass in place of lawn ornaments while a worn mattress leans precariously against the deck. Stairs leading up to the door look unstable at best. A tetanus disaster at worst.

Part of me wishes I could just stuff the letter in the mailbox and leave, but that's not possible. Well, not if I want to keep my job or stay on Melinda's good side, at least. Maybe if I get past this trial period, I won't be the one sent out on middle of the night excursions to tape a paper to someone's door.

"God, why couldn't this have waited til morning?" I mutter, pushing out of my car and slamming the door behind me. My skin prickles, goosebumps running up my forearms and I pause to look up at the house again.

Something feels *wrong*. It feels off here, and not just because the house looks like it should be condemned instead of lived in.

"You're okay," I remind myself, voice flat. "You are so fucking okay it's unreal. It's been a week. You're fine. He doesn't know you're here." I don't want to consider how many times I've repeated that to myself lately, but who cares? There's certainly no one around who might judge me for it. The fear ebbs, though doesn't disappear completely. This place still seems eerie, and some part of my brain wants me to jump back in my car and speed away instead of going up to the door.

But it's just a door, just a house, and just a town at night. I won't let some instinct take over. So with that thought, I make my way across the minefield of a yard and open up the rickety wooden gate that blocks off the front of the deck.

Another shiver travels up my spine, and I hate that I give into my nerves and glance behind me at the still-empty yard.

Well, empty of people, at least. The yard certainly looks terrible, and foreboding. Like a landmine laden field that I'd be likely to either break my leg in or end up with shards of glass embedded in my skin.

How could anyone live like this?

While I've always been on the lower side of middle class, by a lot, it's never been this bad for me. Not since I could personally help it, anyway. My brain reminds me of a foster home long ago where the trash was piled higher than my tiny, emaciated cheeks and hollow eyes.

But that was so many years ago, and not something I could've helped. Now that I'm in charge of myself and my surroundings to some extent, I'd never let my life overflow to this extent. I couldn't, unless I wanted to lose my grip on the sanity I've been hanging onto all these years.

Reaching into my pocket, I unfurl the paper and hold it in both hands. While I'm not sure I'm supposed to look at it, that hasn't stopped me from reading the notice letter that's been printed in bold letters on the front.

From what I can tell, if the Birkins don't want to lose their court appeal for custody, they need to get their act together. But from what I can see here, that ship has sailed and no amount of *getting it together* will do whatever they need it to.

But it isn't my call, and not my case. I'm just here to do whatever Melinda wants from me, then go back to bed and pretend I got a full eight hours instead of five hours broken into pieces.

"Good luck with this making a difference," I mutter, and reach up to slide the paper into the small space between door and frame.

Or at least, that's the plan.

The door swings back some, like it wasn't properly closed, just as a hand rests on the frame beside my face, a body behind me warm and solid.

"I see you're still jumpy in the dark."

Gabriel's voice in my ear makes me nearly levitate and I whirl around, hating that it brings me closer to him instead of further away. "*You*," I hiss, eyes wide.

"It's always me," he promises, eyes sharp in the dim and dingy light from the porch lamp. "And it'll never be anyone else."

He's so close that I could bite him, and his breath is warm against my face. He looks the same as he had a week ago, and a part of me wishes I'd left some kind of mark on him with the coffee mug I'd shattered against his face.

"Shit," I whisper, meeting his eyes. "You're harder to get rid of than a fucking cockroach." For all of my bravado and insults, he terrifies me. Chills run down my spine, and my hands clench at my sides. "How did you find me?"

"The same way I always find you," he replies, leaning forward so his mouth brushes my ear.

"By some dark power you got from selling your soul to the devil?" I ask, voice sharp as I fight not to run screaming from him again.

"By the tracker in your car."

My blood runs cold and I jerk around to look at him, eyes wide and incredulous. "You put a *tracker* in my—" He reaches out and I pull away, my back slamming into the door behind me as my feet take me further from the threat that is Gabriel. I shriek, stumbling, and barely realize I'm on the linoleum of the kitchen instead of the wood of the deteriorating porch. "Leave me alone!"

"Quinn." Worry tinges his sharply handsome features and he follows me, though it only urges me to keep going. "*Quinn*," he says again, this time reaching out and grabbing onto my wrist. "Stop fucking running away from me—"

"I will never stop trying to get away until you leave me the fuck—"

"—*and look behind you.*" He yanks forward on my arm harder than he needs to, causing me to fall into him. For one precarious moment I worry he won't be able to balance both of us, but he straightens and pulls me around, hands on my arms to show me what I've walked into.

"Holy shit," I breathe, eyes fixed on the two dead adults slashed to pieces on the kitchen floor. "Did you—?"

"Never even met them," Gabriel denies, his own words thoughtful. "I guess you didn't go on a slashing spree tonight, either?"

"No, no I definitely didn't. So if it wasn't me, and it wasn't you..." I trail off at the wretched, depraved grin that lights up his eyes and hooks his lips up in an uneven smile.

"Then I think we're trespassing on someone else's territory, little girl. And if I know anything about being a bad person, I doubt he'll like us very much for it." I hate that he slides his arms around my body, holding me more firmly against him.

But even more than that, I hate that I let him.

"God," I mutter, closing my eyes hard instead of looking at the bodies. "I came all this way to get away from you, only to stumble onto this?"

"You're unlucky," Gabriel agrees. "So fucking unlucky. You want to call the cops? We probably should, since you *stepped in their blood and all.*"

CHAPTER
SEVEN

I barely hear what he says when he calls the police.

Instead, I sit down on the rickety deck with nails that are probably full of tetanus sticking out of it, and put my head in my hands with a sigh. Leaving Illinois should have meant leaving all of this behind, but here I am, finding dead bodies with him at my back.

Just like back in Springwood.

I scrub my face when he sits down beside me, immediately moving to get away from him, only for his fingers to grip the back of my shirt and hold me still, like he's scruffing a cat.

"Let's talk about what we're going to say when the cops show up," he tells me evenly, his eyes holding mine in the dim light from the lamp above us. "Don't run away from me. You don't have anywhere to go this time."

"I have so many places to go," I whisper, though the first of them is to a mechanic to get the tracker pulled out of my car... wherever it is. "How dare you *track me*? What's wrong with you, Gabriel? Are you *crazy*?"

His grin turns dark, morbid, and so unsettling that I wish I hadn't asked at all.

"Yeah, Quinn," he murmurs, his grip on my shirt keeping me in place as he leans in close. "I'm insane. That's why I'm here, with you, instead of in any of the other places I'd rather be. Doesn't that make you feel so special? That I'll cross the earth for you without complaint?"

"No," I breathe, heart hammering in my chest. "Let go of me, or I'll hit you."

"Let's talk about that." His other hand comes up and I flinch away, expecting for him to hit me or grab my face harshly.

But he doesn't.

Instead, Gabriel just watches me, and it reminds me of all those times in his office when he'd waited for my fears to pass, or for my anxiety to settle down. He does it now, with his hand inches from my face, and waits for some kind of signal that it's okay to continue.

I hate him for it.

Seconds later, his hand comes to rest on my cheek, and he leans forward so my side is pressed against the wooden rail on my left. "Don't do it again, Quinn. Unless you want me to make you regret it."

"You already make me regret everything," I breathe, eyes fixed on his. "I don't think there's anything else you can do to make this worse."

"There is," he promises. "There are *so* many ways for me to hurt you, and so many of them I'd never even consider. I like it when you fight me." His hand moves to grip my wrist, stopping me from reaching for his throat. Instead, a low chuckle leaves his throat, though his eyes never leave mine. "But if you try to run away again, I'll stop you. I won't let you get nearly as far as you have the last two times."

I don't know what to say to him. My insides flutter, and I can't decide if I'm nauseous or hyperventilating when my breathing picks up and I inhale the scent of his cologne and the leather of his jacket.

"Why did you chase me?" I ask, frozen and trapped on the porch with two dead bodies behind us. They don't bother me nearly as much as him, though. How could they, when they can't do anything to me, and he holds all the power I'd never want him to wield against me? "What do you want, Gabriel?"

He opens his mouth just as sirens sound in the far distance, and disappointment flits across his face. In the next instant, he's on his feet, pulling me up with him to support me on the stairs. "I came here to check on them like I was asked to," he says, voice flat. "We met in the driveway and saw the door was open. You went inside even though I told you not to—"

At my scoff, his grip on my arm tightens, and his mouth twists in a smirk. "You're the more believably naïve one here, Quinn. I came in after you and pulled you back. You almost got sick, you didn't mean to step in the blood. Do you understand me?"

"What if I tell them you did it?" I reply as more of a challenge than a real question.

I expect anger. I expect irritation, at the very least.

But I don't expect the smile that lights up his warm eyes and causes him to shake his head. "Do whatever you want, then," he offers, letting go of me as the cops appear in the driveway. "Do whatever you want, and suffer the consequences." The amusement fades only when the red and blue lights are blinding, and I watch as his face turns serious and official.

It's a perfect mask.

He greets the officers first and I stay behind, looking nervous. His plan is an easy one, and not completely untrue, except for a few key differences. But I go with it, explaining to the cops what had happened and agreeing with Gabriel that we got here at the same time.

"Do you know Dr. Brooks?" the female cop asks, glancing back at my ex-therapist. "I didn't think he was seeing patients just yet."

I don't miss the surreptitious look Gabriel sneaks my way, the question in his eyes, and the way he waits for my answer.

I could do it right here and now. I could tell them the truth, though they may not quite believe me.

I could seal his fate here as being under suspicion. They may not believe me completely, but it would still spell trouble for him if I said something against him. If I told them that he's responsible for other deaths, even if he's cleared of this one.

He couldn't do anything about it, if I told them. Not right here, at least.

"I'd never met him before tonight," I lie, looking up at the woman in earnest. "He told me his name, and that he'd been sent to do a check in, just like I'd been sent with a letter for the front door. We found the door already open, and I..." I trail off, trying to look ashamed and apologetic. "I think I stepped in blood before he had the idea for us to get out of there."

"Weren't you afraid that whoever had done it was still around?" she asks, the sharp sound of stretcher wheels hitting concrete dragging my attention away from her and to the sidewalk behind me.

A body bag is the only thing I see, though. No mangled, torn up body. No wide, staring eyes. Part of me wonders if this is how the Owens family had been carried out of their diner, once Gabriel had been done with them.

Had it been hard to unstick Mr. Owens' face from the grill first?

Nausea rolls in my stomach as I look back up at the

woman. "W-what?" I stammer, needing a moment to process her question. I try to put nerves in my voice, and fear.

She repeats the question, and I fight not to look at Gabriel.

Frankly, the idea of someone more dangerous than him still being here hadn't crossed my mind at all.

After all, how could it?

"I didn't, I'm sorry, I... I was just scared," I lie, trying to sound like I'm confused. "They aren't, right? Whoever did this?"

She hesitates, then shakes her head. "No. We did a thorough search, and it's completely empty. Both of you should go home. If we have any questions, we'll be in touch." The dismissal is as rude as it is cold, and I shrug my shoulders, trying to still look amiable and frightened.

Apparently, I succeed, as the cop pats me awkwardly on the shoulder. "You look pretty worn out," she observes, and I pride myself for selling the act. "Are you all right to drive home?"

"I'll take her home," Gabriel offers, sounding a few degrees different from how he normally speaks to me. His eyes are earnest, his posture less sure of himself and more modest. This isn't the real Gabriel, or the one I know from Springwood.

This is an act, and a damn good one.

"No, it's okay," I say quickly, kicking myself for selling the act so well. "I don't mind driving myself home. It isn't far, just across town. Thirty minutes or so," I promise, hoping she believes me.

But she doesn't, and she trades a look with the other cop.

I'm not a child, damn it, I want to snap. *Stop treating me like one.*

"I'll take her home," Gabriel says again, pressing the solution into their brains so they're more likely to accept it. He tosses me a warning glance and I press my lips together, knowing that if I push the issue further, it'll look suspicious.

Neither of us needs to look suspicious right now.

"But I need my car to go to work tomorrow," I point out, vocalizing a very real issue.

"I'll take it back," the woman offers, holding out a hand for my keys. "I go that way, anyway. Really, I think it's better for him to drive you home. You look exhausted, and I don't think it's a good idea for you to drive."

I'm *fine*, but I finally only nod and hand my keys to her like any part of me is grateful.

I'm not.

How could I be, when Gabriel reaches out to gesture in the direction of his car and walks toward it with one last, grateful word with both cops.

"I'd rather walk," I say finally, when we're far enough away that only he'll hear me. All I get is a snort, and him opening the passenger door of a black Camaro.

Of course, his car is much nicer than mine.

Hesitating, I look inside and my knees suddenly lock at the idea of getting into a car with him. I'll be trapped.

I'll be alone with *him*. There won't be a way for me to protect myself, and he could just take off with me like I'm sure he wants to.

He could kill me, even. No one would be able to stop him, and—

"Breathe, Quinn." His voice in my ear, soft and almost sweet, is unexpected. So is the hand on my elbow and his solid warmth behind me. "If I wanted to hurt you, I would. I know where you live, remember? I could've hurt you any night that you've been here, and it would've been a lot easier than getting your blood all over my car."

I shudder, feeling his breath on my neck, just under my ear. "Is that supposed to be comforting?" I snap in a voice that shakes for real.

He chuckles. "Yeah, it is. And it's meant to get you in the car before either of our cop friends comes over to see what's wrong. Don't make this harder than it has to be, all right?"

With those words I force my body to cooperate, reminding myself that he's right, and that he could've done a lot worse than this by now if he'd wanted to. Still, it's difficult.

I've been in enough dangerous situations for my body to recognize another one, and it takes all of my willpower to sit in the front seat of his fancy car and buckle my seatbelt with cold fingers that shake.

By the time I'm done, he's in the car as well, the engine running softly as he looks at me. When I meet his eyes, my gaze narrows, and I fix him with all the dislike and vitriol in one look as I can manage. As if he needs to be reminded about how I feel about him.

But all he does is scoff.

He doesn't talk on the way to my newly rented house. He doesn't say a word until he's pulled into my driveway and turned the engine off, the lights off and throwing our surroundings into darkness.

"Thanks," I mutter, feeling like politeness is the bare minimum, and pull the door open.

Or at least, I try to.

Nothing happens, and when I try again, my heart slams into my ribs at the realization of being trapped.

"Gabriel—" I yank on the door handle again, putting my entire body into it like it'll make a difference. At this point, though, I have a better chance of breaking the door than unlocking it, and Gabriel doesn't seem at all upset about the possibility.

"Can I come in?" he asks airily, like I'm not fighting with the door.

"Of course not. Let me *out*—" The lock pops open and I

50

nearly fall out of the car when the door suddenly swings back on its frame.

I swear I hear him laugh, just as I hear his own door closing and see him walk amiably up towards my small porch.

"No, I said *no!*" I remind him, catching up to him and over-taking him on the porch, right in front of my door. The small area is mostly covered, granting me privacy from my neighbors, and right now, it's that fact that works against me.

Gabriel shoves me backward, until my back is against the door and his hands are on either side of me, fingers splayed on the glass. With no light from my porch and nothing to see his expression by, I can only go by his breath on my lips and the warmth from his body, for all the good that does.

"I said you couldn't come in," I remind him, a tremor in my voice that I try to chase away. "I said—"

"I'm worried for you," he says, cutting me off in the middle of my reminder. "Seriously, Quinn. I know how hard this was for you back home. I know you went back into therapy with someone else." He can't hide the disdain at it being not with him, and I nearly snort with dark amusement at his jealousy. "Talk to me."

"I want you to leave," I say when given a chance.

But he only snickers, and suddenly I feel his hand on my chest, just below my collarbone. "I won't hurt you," he reminds me, as confusion muddles my thoughts and freezes me in place. "I have never wanted to hurt you. Why do you keep running from me, Quinn?"

His hand slides up, gently, until his fingers are close to my throat and I tilt my head back to create space from his touch. "Then what do you want? To *help*?" I spit in his face. "Don't make me—"

"I want *you*."

The words are frank, honest, and I can't move when he says

them. I feel stricken, like a deer in headlights, but there's no light here and it's his words that have me paralyzed.

"What?" I ask, sure I've heard him wrong.

"I want... *you*." His fingers close around my throat, cradling it gently. "From the first time you opened up to me in my office and showed me how sweet you are, and how funny. From the first time I killed for you, it's always been *you*, Quinn."

"No." I swallow underneath his fingers, and wish I had more than one-word answers in me. I'm not supposed to be afraid of anything, and even if he is the only exception, I'm not the type of person to let him do this and stand here like a victim.

I have to do something.

Anything.

"Aren't you tired of running from me?" he goes on, his face so close to mine that I feel the brush of his unshaven skin against my cheek. "When are you going to let me show you how I feel?"

"When you're dead," I say, trying to find my voice. "Or when I'm dead. But I don't think we're going to the same place afterward, so—"

"Are you so sure about that?" He certainly doesn't seem perturbed by my words, but I refuse to let them sink in.

"You're a murderer," I remind him. "You killed the Owens—"

"I've killed a lot more people than that."

The words stun me. My breath catches in my chest, just as his fingers tighten until he's half-restricting my breathing, and I feel him with every bit of air that enters my lungs. "You're not really shocked, are you?" he taunts, and I hate that I am. It had been almost romantic, if a bit deranged, to think that he'd become a murderer for me.

But to know that it's just part of *him*, and that they weren't the only ones?

That's another ballpark entirely.

"Let go," I order, trying to sound anything other than terrified.

"Or what?"

"Or I'll break the glass door and stab you in the throat, Gabriel."

He laughs. I've always loved his laugh, but the tinge of madness it holds makes me shiver and close my eyes hard against the implications.

"You're not even lying, are you?" he snickers, and his face is back to being too close, his breath hot against my parted lips. "I'd love to see you try, but not tonight. Not now. Not when you need to sleep and figure out what you're going to tell your boss tomorrow. Try not to panic, Quinn. Remember how I told you to relax and—"

"Shut up, *shut up!*" I slam my hands into him, but he doesn't let go of my throat, and barely moves away. "You're not my therapist anymore! *Shut up!*"

"Maybe not, but I still know you better than anyone ever could," he points out, his other hand reaching out to grip my hip so sharply that I open my mouth in a surprised gasp.

It's what he's waiting for. Gabriel strikes, his mouth finding mine and pressing until I'm shoved against the door once more. My hands fall, one of them finding the door handle, and before I can stop to think about what I'm doing, my teeth close on his lower lip. *Hard.*

Gabriel snarls, a sound I've never heard from him, but instead of pulling away, he leans forward so his body is a solid line against mine, one of his knees pressing between my thighs. Warmth floods me, and heat sinks to a spot under my stomach, close to where his body rubs against mine.

But I refuse to think about that, or do more than acknowledge it. I bite down harder, until I taste blood, and finally he jerks away, clearly in pain.

Then Gabriel *laughs*. He sounds insane as I grope for the door handle again and step to the side so I can open it. He touches his lip, and in the dim light, I can barely see him swipe his tongue across the bite, still snickering.

"I always knew you'd like to play," he tells me, lifting his head as if trying to find my eyes in the dark. "I always knew, Quinn—"

I don't let him finish the sentence. Instead, I slam the door in his face, locking it and checking every window and door in the house before escaping to the bathroom, turning on the shower, and escaping into the hot water surrounded by darkness.

CHAPTER

EIGHT

W hen I'm not dreaming of him, I'm dreaming of
something worse.

Sometimes, it's just the feeling of a worse time, as
opposed to one of the terrible things that had happened to me
in foster care.

Tonight, it's the former, though I'm surprised that it isn't
Gabriel when he's always so close to my thoughts lately.

In my thin, worn sneakers I walk along the dark hallway, my
shoulders trembling under the threadbare cardigan I wear. If I could
just change this one decision, so many other bad nights might have
not happened.

I'm thirteen, and in my fourth foster home. This one is worse
than the last, and all I want is to be free from here, no matter what it
takes.

They hate me, the thought echoes in my brain, planting itself
there with surety. My foster parents actively despise me, rather than
just dismissing me like the others. They only want the money from
the state, not to take care of us. For the most part, the seven other
kids and I take care of ourselves.

The door creaks open to my left and I stop, eyes wide, to meet the eyes of the other girl who lives here. Sylvie shakes her head, face drawn and frightened. "Don't," she whispers. "They'll catch you, Quinn. They won't let you leave."

"I'd rather die than stay," I reply, so sure, even at thirteen, that my only options are death or escape. I'd seen what had happened to her.

I'd seen the times that our foster father had crept into her room, and how much she cried afterward. While it hadn't happened to me, I had promised myself that it wouldn't, one way or another.

I creep onward, making my way down the stairs as she closes her door and presumably creeps back to bed. I'd asked for her to come with me, but she'd told me that she couldn't.

She was too afraid.

It was a fair point, seeing as our foster father was mean. He hurt the boys and girls alike, and everyone went to their rooms the moment he came home, lest we trigger his drunken irritation before he oozed all the alcohol from his pores by yelling at his wife.

I can't do it anymore. The thought echoes across my thoughts, and my eyes fall on the front door that's nestled up to the kitchen counter. I don't know where I'll go. I don't care, really. As long as it isn't here.

"Where are you going, Quinn?" The voice shocks me to a standstill. Fear causes my throat to close, and slowly I turn to look up and up at the imposing, terrifying figure of my foster father.

"Nowhere," I whisper, my body shaking like a leaf in a thunderstorm. "Nowhere, I was just—"

"Don't you lie to me. Don't you dare—" He takes a step forward, only to stop with a choked off gasp. Metal claws stab through his chest, and from over his shoulder, Gabriel looks at me with pity, empathy, and worry.

"I'll keep you safe, Quinn," he murmurs, pulling the long blades back through my foster father's chest.

I can't do anything but stare at them. I can't do anything but watch as Gabriel stabs my cruel foster father over and over again, until he slumps to the ground and his blood spreads toward me like reaching fingers.

When I step back and look at Gabriel, the fear is gone and I'm no longer thirteen. I'm twenty-three, and the house from my childhood has morphed into the house I'd seen the two dead bodies in only a few days ago.

There are lines on Gabriel's face that weren't there when I'd met him in Springwood, and I don't stop him as he steps forward to cup my cheek in the hand he doesn't wear his claws on. "I'll keep you safe. I won't let you do anything you regret."

"I've never done anything like that," I murmur, confusion sparking in my brain as he cradles my face and leans down, lips brushing mine. "Gabriel, what do you mean?" He kisses me, and in my dream it's the softest brush of his mouth against mine, just enough to have me on my tiptoes and begging for more.

"You know what I mean." He draws back and picks up my hand, where I'm suddenly holding a sharp, thin blade that glitters in the light from the window. Blood stains the metal and my fingers, and I drop it with a gasp, a question on my lips—

When I sit up, shaking, I'm surprised the force isn't enough to send me through the window on the other side of the small bedroom. I groan and bury my face in my hands, dragging my knees up to press my body against them.

"Fuck," I mutter, running the dream over and over through my brain. It does no good, though. No matter how many times I try to figure out what he meant, I can't. Worse, the dream shreds when I scrutinize it, blowing away my thoughts in the storm outside.

I've dreamed of my past before, but never with Gabriel taking center stage unless it was about him specifically. That night had happened before I'd ever met him, and it unfortunately hadn't ended in Gabriel saving me.

My foster father had hurt me, though thankfully not in the same way he liked to hurt Sylvie. He'd broken my arm, and when I'd put myself in front of him a week later to protect Sylvie, social services had no choice but to intervene.

Though I'd never been told what had happened to Sylvie.

I turn to look at the window, unsurprised to see that the sun is well and risen. With my schedule, sleeping past dawn is a given. A storm pounds against the window, and I shiver as I curl back up under the thick comforter I'd brought with me from my dorm room. I don't have to get up just yet, and as much as I hate it, I still can't get the dream and Gabriel out of my head. Though hopefully pouring a mug of coffee down my throat and inhaling a bunch of cereal will go a long way toward getting rid of him from my thoughts.

IT's NOT that I dislike my job.

It's that Clara, the woman who shares my cubicle, is insufferable. For three days she's talked about the double homicide, chatting my ear off as I try to work through my pile of cases while she comes up with multiple theories about what could have happened.

Any part of it that was entertaining is gone, and whenever she sits down and rolls her squeaky chair close to mine, I have to fight the urge to get up and leave. "I heard they have a lead," she whispers conspiratorially in my ear, like she's letting me in on some kind of secret. "Did you hear me, Quinn?"

How could I not, when she's close enough to wheeze against my face?

"Yeah, I heard you." I sigh, putting down my pen and looking up at her. A part of me wants to reach out and push her away on her squeaky chair to give myself some space, but that would be wrong. It would not be building the *workplaces cama- raderie* that Melinda is so fond of, and I'm sure that should mean something to me too.

At the very least, I have to pretend it does.

"Aren't you interested? I know you're not from around here, but you *found* the bodies with Dr. Brooks." She sighs and looks away, her eyes filled with what are probably thoughts of Dr. Brooks himself.

I have to admit, he's easy to have a crush on. He's easy to like, with his winning personality and inviting charm. He's kind, understanding, and the therapist everyone would line up to see.

But it's a mask. A very good one, but the real Gabriel Brooks isn't just those things.

He's a monster.

But hey, more power to Clara if she wants to get on his bad side or bring down his ire on her. It'll give me more space to spread out, and the peace and quiet I thrive in. Though I somehow don't think he'd kill my coworker. Unfortunately for me.

"Aren't you off in..." I check my phone, and try not to praise the lord in relief. "Thirty-two seconds?" But who's counting? Certainly not me.

"I'm sticking around for a few minutes," Clara says shyly, smoothing down her blonde hair and glancing toward the door. "Melinda has a meeting."

"What does that have to do with you?" She tosses me a confused, possibly offended look, as if she can't figure out if I'm being mean. So I fix the brightest smile on my face I can manage, to appease her.

It works, though I'm not certain I don't look like I'm having some sort of stroke. As she speaks again, I relax my face, hoping it won't get stuck like that if I have to do it often, for Clara's sake.

"Melinda has a meeting," she explains, fidgeting on her chair. "I just thought I'd stick around. Maybe she needs some help, or..." She shrugs her shoulders as I survey her face in confusion. Clara's never this anxious. Like she wants the meeting to happen, but also doesn't.

"Is it about you?" I ask, wondering if she's at risk of getting fired. While I haven't heard any office whispers about her having a poor performance, I also don't know if I'd ever be privy to them. I'm an *outsider,* after all.

Clara opens her mouth to speak just as the door opens, the small bell sounding gently through the office as my lips press together in a thin line.

Gabriel stands at the entrance to the office, looking around with polite interest as he steps inside and gently closes the door behind him. He clears his throat like he's feeling awkward, or just out of place, and takes off his jacket to hang it on the hook beside the door before his eyes search the room and land on me.

Unlike Clara, who's trying her best to get his attention and look good doing it, I couldn't be less happy about his presence. He cocks a brow at me, but I don't give an inch. I only glare, and mentally urge him back out to whence he came, so my heart can slow down and my fingers can unclench from my pen.

I'm afraid of him. There's nothing to stop the thought from echoing across my thoughts, and I can't help the small shiver that travels down my spine. For all the false bravado I show when he's bothering me, I can't hide it right now.

Gabriel Brooks terrifies me just as much as he drags my unwilling interest toward him. He's gorgeous today, as he is every day. As I watch, he runs a hand through his light brown hair and smiles at Clara.

"Hello there," he greets in his sweet, warm voice. "Do you know where Mrs. Melinda's office is?" Is that a trace of southern charm I hear, just to please the people around him?

Most likely.

"Yeah, she's back here." Clara pushes into his space, smiling and trying to get his full attention. He gives it reluctantly, and allows her to lead him through the office to Melinda's small corner room while I shake my head and go back to my work.

It's no use, though.

The fact that he's here means I can't concentrate, and even though Clara isn't talking to me anymore, she's still existing in my periphery, jumping at the chance to catch him as he comes out. My stomach knots and unknots, no matter how many deep breaths I take, until finally I'm a flinching mess at my desk and I give up, burying my face in my hands.

The door opens from somewhere behind me, but I don't move. Not while Clara twitters at him, or while he responds to her politely, yet distantly. He doesn't like her, if I had to guess. But that's not exactly a shock.

"Give me a second, please?" he says, firmly but kindly, and I jump when I realize he's closer to me than I'd expected. "I'd like to check on Quinn." I look up at him as he says it, the action reminding me of my dream when I'd been so small, looking up and up into the face of—

"You look tired," he murmurs, leaning down over my desk. "Are you not sleeping, Quinn?" There's worry in his eyes, and a predatory gleam that I'm pretty sure he reserves just for me.

"I'm fine," I snap, wishing he wasn't so close. "I'm sleeping fine." It's not quite true, and my gaze falls to the desk, where I'm clutching my pen, as I say it.

"What's wrong?" he asks, voice still so soft. "You can tell me—"

"It's nothing you can help me with," I interrupt, wishing I was half as brave as I'm trying to sound. The effect is lost, however, by my trembling hands that I know he sees as well. His hand comes out, and he covers my fingers, stilling the trembling as he waits for me to go on. "It's just nightmares, okay? It's not—"

"I got that number you were asking for." Clara's back, and her eyes fall on our hands, then jump up to my face. Her eyes narrow at the contact as I snatch my hands away, putting them on my lap and away from him as he straightens with a sigh.

"Thank you so much," he replies, taking the business card from her. From the corner of my eye I see that along with some other number, Clara's name and number are written on the card. She's desperate for the wrong man, and I'm not about to be the one to tell her. "I'll see you ladies later, all right?" He winks at Clara, and it's so cheesy I feel like vomiting.

But not Clara. She sucks in a breath and looks at him with wide, adoring eyes as he walks out the door, her hands clutching the notepad in her fingers as he goes. "Do you think he'll call me?" she asks, glancing my way. "I think he'll call me."

"Yeah, Clara," I agree, trying to refocus on the pile of work in front of me. "He's totally going to call you."

CHAPTER

NINE

It's happening again.

My feet are bare this time, and I stare down the hallway to the stairs where lights are on downstairs. My foster father is screaming, and my name on his lips means terrible things for me.

His silhouette throws the landing into shadow, and I hear my name again, this time with a threat as his steps seem to shake the house. He ascends one step, then another, and I slide down the wall on the opposite side, hands covering my head. Soon enough he's at the top, walking towards me with threats that cause me to tremble, and I can feel the moment he reaches out—

I sit up hard. A gasp ripping from my throat and the nightmare eats at me as the hand on my shoulder tightens—

"Quinn." The voice isn't my foster father's. It chases away the dream until I'm blinking in the soft darkness of my room and staring up into a face I don't immediately recognize.

It takes two blinks and for my heart to nearly stop until I jerk backward. Then I shove Gabriel at the same time and pull a sigh from him as he barely budges.

"What are you doing here?" I shriek, trying to get off the

bed and instead tangling myself in my blankets. "How did you get in here?!"

"Watching you sleep. And saving you from nightmares," Gabriel replies coolly, rubbing his arm where I'd hit him. "You were having a rough time. What was your dream about?"

"You," I lie, my heart speeding up until it feels like it's trying to rocket me out of here. "I dreamed of you, doing shit like this—" I try to roll out of the bed, only for him to be faster. He lunges, until he's situated above me and somehow, by some stroke of bad luck, there are no longer blankets between us.

It's just him, in his perfect jeans and his black v-neck tee, and me in my tee shirt and running shorts. For a moment he just stares at me, and the breath catches in my throat as I feel his eyes wander down my body.

I don't want this. The thought echoes through my brain, and I struggle under him only to hear a soft sound, like a growl coming from the man above me.

Except, it isn't a growl. I realize that when his lips part and the chuckle bubbles up from between them. His mouth curls into a half-grin, rueful for all that it's charming. "I love watching you sleep, Quinn," he admits, not caring that I'm still struggling. Instead, he moves to sit on my hips, pinning me down with his weight. "You make the sweetest faces when you dream. It's so hard not to do something about it."

"Do... something?" I repeat, my voice soft. "You mean—"

"It doesn't matter what I mean." Is he irritated that he's said it? A frown crosses his features, but is chased away quickly by amusement once more. "I came here to save you from your nightmares. No matter how not-real they are. Talk to me, baby girl. What are you dreaming of that's keeping you tossing and turning all night?"

"All night?" I repeat again, like a parrot. "If you're so concerned, why not wake me up before this?"

"I have," he sighs, one hand coming up to stroke my face. I flinch away, though his touch doesn't sear my skin or hurt like I wish it would.

His fingers are warm against my face, and trail lightly until I want to shudder under him. His nails are a sharp, pleasant sensation as he strokes up one of my cheeks, across my nose, and down the other before repeating the process.

"I don't remember—"

"It barely took anything the other times," he interrupts. "And you didn't really wake up. You just curled up with me again and let me hold you as you went back to sleep. Like I said, Quinn. You're just so sweet when you're asleep."

My heart pounds and I look anywhere but at him. I don't move, as if that'll just entice him to hurt me, but I have no idea what to do, or how to get him to leave.

He's been here all night?

I'm never going to sleep again.

"What's hurting you so badly in your sleep?" Gabriel asks again in a voice reminiscent of his therapist tone. "Talk to me."

"Why?" It's probably irrelevant, and his brows raise in the dim light from the moon that filters through the thin, cheap curtains on the window.

"Because I'm going to help you."

"I don't think you can," I snap, trying to sound like I neither want his help, nor think he'll be of any use. He won't, I don't think. I'm sure he can't help me. Not with this.

"I was so good at helping you before." When I try to bolt upright, his hand is suddenly at my throat, pushing me backward until my head is back on the pillow and all I can do is glare up at him. "Don't make me keep grabbing you," he suggests. "I'm not trying to be rough tonight. Besides, what do you have to lose?"

Images flicker through my head, of the bodies in the diner,

of more bodies with shadowed faces that represent other people he's killed.

How many have there been?

"I've been dreaming about my foster homes," I admit hesitantly, and his grip loosens on my throat. "I don't know. Maybe it's this job. It's what I've always wanted to do. To *help* kids in my situation, or stop people from doing... you know." The only good thing is that I don't need to elaborate. He's heard this all before from me, and he knows about my past. "But every night now I dream of the bad house. The one with all the other kids." He knows about this too. He knows, because he worked with my social worker and she'd told him the details.

"What are the dreams like?" It's easier when I don't look at him. I can pretend it isn't *this* Gabriel that's helping me. I can, instead, pretend that it's Dr. Brooks, the therapist who had done so much for me when I was a teenager.

The one I'd had a secret, taboo crush on. I'd been secure in my knowledge that he'd never like me back. He was too old for me. Too established and successful.

Too *nice*, younger me had thought.

"I'll tell you if you let go of my throat," I say finally, feeling like I need some kind of bargaining chip here. My heart beats normally, as it should, and I take long breaths of air to try to calm the rest of me.

While he's the demon of my dreams who's never gone from them for very long, the unfortunate truth is that everything he likes to remind me of is true.

He's never hurt me.

I have a million reasons to be afraid of him, and one reason not to that never seems to want to go away. Gabriel Brooks has never hurt *me*.

Just declared that I'm his, killed multiple people for me, and followed me from town to town for the last five years.

No big deal or anything.

"I want to sit up," I add, after a few moments of tense silence. He hesitates, and I don't think he's going to let me do it. He likes his control too much, I think. His power over me to—

Gabriel sits back smoothly, reaching a hand out to pull me up once he's off of my legs entirely. I don't take it, because I'm not an idiot. I sit up on my own, knees pulled up to my chest as I eye him warily.

"Don't you sleep?" I ask. "You're not a fucking vampire, are you?"

"I sleep," he assures me, amusement crossing his face. "But I'm a night owl by nature. I don't mind staying up for you."

"I don't need it."

"Tell me about your dreams."

My eyes flick down to the bed, and I mentally unravel the small knotted thread sticking out from the edge of the sheet until my hand snakes down to it so I can run my nail across the bump in the fabric.

This, too, reminds me so much of our therapy sessions, though not in a great way. He'd always pushed me to tell him the things that had made me uncomfortable, and I had always balked and bitched about it.

Tonight doesn't feel any different.

"First, I kept dreaming of the night I tried to run away." The words feel like they're being dragged from me, and I reach out to turn on the lamp by my pillow in order to see his face better.

It's a mistake, of course. Because that just reminds me how much I enjoy looking at him, and the fact that he's nice *to* look at. I chalk it up to another relic from teen-Quinn who didn't know any better, and push it to the side.

"Of getting caught, and when I broke my arm. But..." I

don't like admitting the rest of it; that Gabriel had shown up in those dreams on and off. "But I don't like that dream," I lie instead, keeping my voice cool and even.

"Does it happen the same as when you were little?" he pulls his knees up to his chest as well, as if he's mirroring my pose. "Dreams are rarely perfect memories. What things change?"

You.

Licking my bottom lip, I try to look like I'm remembering. "I don't know," I lie instead, shrugging my shoulders under the thin cotton of my tee. "I don't remember them so well. Lately, it's another night. After that, or maybe before. It's more general, and my foster father from the bad house is coming to find me." My voice falters as fear spikes through my chest just at the memory.

I hate it; the feeling of weakness, of helplessness. And I hate remembering all the things that had happened, when—

"And what aren't you telling me?"

He had always been so good at that, that I shouldn't be surprised nothing has changed. I roll my eyes at him, wishing I could distract him from what I don't want to say. "For someone *not* in my dreams, you like to think you're skilled at figuring out what's in them," I say coldly, a brittle edge to my tone. "There's nothing else—"

"I'm going to tell you a secret, Quinn." Gabriel moves until he's sitting beside me, and reaches out slowly to pick up my hand. "Do you see this?" His grip is light, though his skin is so warm on mine that it takes me a moment to realize what he means.

I blink at his hand, then at mine, but I don't see anything except my fingers. "My... hand?" I ask, wondering if maybe he *has* lost it.

Gabriel sighs, and slides his grip down until he can hold my thumb up between us.

The skin around my nail is bleeding.

The sight of it seems to trigger the pain, and small prickles of sharpness assaults my senses, making me flex the offending digit. "Okay?" I ask, still not quite understanding what he's getting at.

"You do this when you're upset. When you're *lying*, normally. Anytime you're trying to tell a lie, you rip at the skin around your nails. You haven't changed much in five years, and I can still read you like a book." He drops my hand with a grin; but doesn't pull away from me.

Instead, before I can move, he's on me again. Pressing me back against the bed as I sink down until my head is on the pillow with his fingers around my throat again.

"I asked you not to—" I begin, but he cuts me off with a sneer.

"You lost your privileges when you lied until I had to call you out on it. *Stay*, Quinn." He isn't sitting on me to hold me down this time, but I'm not sure I could break free of his grip if I tried.

Still, my hand flies up to grip his forearm, and under my grip, I can feel the flex of his muscles as he holds me in place. Experimentally, I try to pull him away, but just as I'd expected, there's no way in hell I'm getting him off of me.

My heart speeds up, bile rising in my throat, but he doesn't do a thing except watch me.

"Tell me the rest," Gabriel orders in a soft purr that's *nothing* like his therapy voice. "And I'll let you sit up."

"I dream of you," I gasp, when his fingers tighten around my airway. They don't stop, though. His face remains impassive, filled with casual interest, and his finger and thumb slide to press just under my jaw until the world is spinning and I'm trying to get him off of me in earnest.

I should've run the moment he let me up.

"I'm not lying! It's you, it's *always you.* But no—not like that." His grip loosens ever so slightly, and the world stops spinning. "You always show up before... before the bad part. Before he hurts me. You show up and you kill him, then I'm older and not a kid anymore—" He shifts, moving his other arm toward my face, and I flinch.

"Shh," Gabriel murmurs, dragging his knuckles down my cheek. "Don't flinch away from me. I haven't hurt you." The discomfort in my neck begs to differ, and the way my world is still spinning.

But he's right.

It doesn't hurt. My heart pounds and butterflies do laps in my stomach, but it's not from pain or fear this time, though more than anything I wish it was.

Instinctively I press my thighs together, wide eyes still on his, and I see the moment his attention is dragged downward, his touch on my face stilling as he realizes what I'm doing.

"No," I say, before he can speak. "I know what you think—"

"You don't know what I think," Gabriel assures me, a quick smile crossing his lips. "But I have a pretty good idea of what's going through *your* mind right now. It's not strange to like it, you know."

"I didn't like it," I promise as he pulls his hand away from my face. He's so close right now that I can smell his cologne, sharp like frost in my nose. "I don't like any of this, or you, or—"

"So you dream of me killing your foster father at the bad house." He shifts until he's leaning over me, and my breath catches in my throat when he splays a hand against my stomach. "How do I do it?"

"You stab him," I reply, unable to stop replaying the dream over and over in my head.

"And how does it feel when you watch me do it? Do you want to help? Would you rather it be you killing him, instead of me?"

I open my mouth to reply, and pause. Because I don't know. I've never thought about it, I realize. I've never stopped to analyze how I *feel* about Gabriel killing the man that had made a year and some change of my life the worst thing I've ever encountered.

But now that I *am* thinking about it, I can't stop. I shudder when his hand slips upward, under my shirt, but even that isn't enough to pull my thoughts away from my dreams completely. "I don't know," I say finally. "But I know that when you do, everything feels so real. It's like I snap out of some kind of trance, and I don't have to follow the memory anymore—" I grip his wrist, eyes flicking to his and narrowing. "No," I say firmly, and he just watches me, his hand stilling.

"You're afraid you'll like it," Gabriel accuses, but I don't have anything to say back to him.

We both know it's true, after all.

Instead, I struggle to sit up again, and I'm surprised when he lets me. A breath leaves me and I get to my feet, hands shaking and my thumb throbbing, now that he's brought attention to it. "Leave me alone," I snap, pointing towards the door. "And get out of my house. Get your *own* fucking house."

"I already have one," Gabriel assures me, running his fingers through his tousled hair. "It's a lot nicer than yours, and has better beds. Come over sometime. I don't mind showing you."

Instead of answering, I flip him off. He watches me, then snorts and gives a quick shake of his head. "You're asking for it," he informs me, on his way to the door. It's not until he gets there, however, and it's half open, that he stops and turns to look at me, gaze softening ever so slightly.

"Don't forget what I said," he reminds me, and I roll my eyes in fearful exasperation.

"That you'll never hurt me? I *get it*—"

"No, Quinn." He waits patiently until I look up at him again. "Not that part. The part about you belonging to me. Maybe if you understand that, it won't come as a shock one of these days when you wake up and find me in your bed. Or better, maybe you'll wake up in *mine*."

He takes the moment that mind is trying to process that to grin and leave, closing the door hard behind him. Even from inside I hear him whistling as he goes down the driveway, and it isn't until I can't hear him anymore that I let out a breath and collapse onto the floor, burying my face in my hands and wondering if this is another nightmare I'll wake up from soon.

CHAPTER

TEN

There's something insanely cathartic about Carla's swooning, Melinda's worry, and the man in front of me who's currently screaming me down like I'm forty feet away, instead of four inches.

I take in a breath and look around to see Carla's stricken face and the absence of anyone else in the office. If Melinda is here, then she's doing a good job of not showing her face.

The problem, for the balding six-foot-five man with muscles that probably haven't come from the gym, is that I'm not afraid of him.

At all.

My fingers drum on my coffee mug as he screams, and I pull it out of the way to prevent any of his spit from landing in my hours old coffee. He continues, boasting more lung capacity than I'd expected, until finally I look away, bored with the show.

"It wasn't my call, Mr. Durham," I point out, when he inevitably stops to suck in oxygen. "I've only been your case worker for what? Three days?" My brows raise, and I search for a silent insult that fits how I feel about Melinda dumping *another* case on me. It's the third in the time I've been here, and I'm starting to wonder if it's becoming a permanent trend. "The decision to take away what was left of your custody had nothing to do with me. And if you wanted some kind of help from me, you shouldn't be here screaming. It makes me even less likely to help you; if we're being honest with each other."

I lean back in my chair, waiting for his next rant.

It's shorter than I expect, and I sip my coffee as it winds down. "Yeah, now I'm really not looking to make your case a priority. I'm not a big fan of name-calling, Mr. Durham." Before he can start again, I add, "Please leave before I have to call the police. I think both of us have better things to do today, don't you?" While he doesn't scare me, his unpredictability and the way he shifts back and forth in front of my desk make me nervous.

If I take away all of his options, will he try to hurt me? If I'm the one to snuff out his hope of ever getting his child back, even on every other weekend, will he flip over this desk and try to strangle the life out of me?

It's possible, though that still doesn't make me fear him.

"You're going to be sorry you've done this to me," he utters, his frame shaking like a leaf in the wind. It isn't fear, and it isn't worry.

He hates me. He *blames* me, though we've gone over the fact that it's not my fault and, frankly, the blame lies with him.

After all, I'm not the one who got drunk and hit his wife multiple times before moving on to selling drugs for extra money.

"I haven't done anything to you," I remind him, tilting my head back and closing my eyes to hide the eye roll that I can't avoid. "But I'll look into your case, if you would leave and stop yelling at me. I can't actually *do my job* with you here, after all."

He holds my gaze and I refuse to look away, though the sound-track of Clara's nervous, heavy breathing behind me is enough to make me fidget a little.

Finally he shoves away from the desk, not saying anything as he storms out of the office and disappears past the front window.

Clara lets out a long, nervous breath and sags back in her chair, just as Melinda appears from the staff room as if she'd really been there the whole time, organizing or doing something else that wasn't *hiding*.

"You were so good at acting like you weren't afraid," Clara remarks as Melinda wanders over. My boss frowns at the door, then at me.

"Everything all right, Quinn?" she asks, her wrinkled face drawn. "I heard the commotion from the staff room. I was wondering if I should call the cops."

I shrug, not telling her that, honestly, calling the cops wouldn't have hurt the situation. In fact, having an automatic out would've been nice. My fingers drum on the coffee mug once more, and I shrug my shoulders like I'm just pushing away the experience. And maybe I am.

"It was Mr. Durham. He's... upset," I tell my boss, wondering how much of the conversation she'd heard. Most of it, I'd assume. I'm sure people down the street heard it too, considering the volume of the man's yelling. "It's fine. I'm handling it." Though I don't add, *I wish you hadn't put me on his case*, still meeting her gaze squarely. *I wish you'd let me do something that's not so high stakes.*

"Well, I'm sure you'll take care of it." That she pawns off cases she doesn't like on us doesn't thrill me, but at least she's willing to take responsibility for us. Melinda's words are accompanied by a forced, tight smile, and she turns to me with a softness in her eyes that I don't expect. "Why don't you take off early today, Quinn? It's slow, and you look like you're almost done." She surveys my desk as I set the coffee cup down, surprised.

"Oh... yeah?" I ask, more than a little taken aback. "If you want me to?"

"You deserve a night off. Maybe there's someone in town who you'll find to hold your interest?" She reminds me of the southern aunt in some old movie when she says it with a meaningful look, and I fight not to roll my eyes. Instead, a smirk crawls up over my lips, and I shake my head.

"I'm not really looking for anything," I admit, getting to my feet with a pile of work. "Not right now."

"Not even with our charming new therapist? Dr. Brooks is working with us now, you know. It wouldn't hurt to get to know him a little better." Melinda glances at me knowingly, her lips pursed.

Behind me, I can feel Clara radiating disapproval. If either of us is dying to get to know Dr. Brooks better, it's definitely not me.

"Oh, Melinda," my coworker chuckles sharply. "I think Dr. Brooks is a little old for Quinn, don't you?"

"Not really," Melinda shrugs. "I know when I was young, I was always interested in distinguished older men. What do you think?" She looks at me, and with a jolt, I realize it isn't a rhetorical question.

"Err..." I blink, trying to find anywhere else to look as my stomach twists into a knot. "No, I... I don't know what my type is." That's a dumb answer. It's stupid, and I wince slightly. "I mean, I don't think it's Gabri—Dr. Brooks." *Damn it.* Calling him by his first name isn't going to convince them, and sure enough, Melinda looks up with triumph shining in her eyes.

If I'm not careful, her confidence is going to get me shot by Clara.

"Anyway, I really appreciate the night off," I say hurriedly, dropping my finished files into a wire basket. "Thank you, Melinda. I'll see you guys tomorrow?" They agree; with Melinda seeing me off with much more goodwill than the angry, clearly irritated Clara.

Well, it's not my fault she has bad taste in men, or that she thinks I want anything to do with Gabriel.

That's what I tell myself, as I try not to think about his hands on my thighs, or his voice in my ear after he'd woken me up from my nightmares a few days ago. It had been more helpful than I'll ever admit. Especially since my nightmares had been chased away by his touch and his scent.

But I refuse to let him be my savior this time.

I'm so wrapped up in my thoughts as I walk down toward the parking lot that I don't notice the man standing in the hedges until Mr. Durham is stepping forward, his fingers gripping my sleeves hard.

"What—" I break off with a sharp intake of breath, eyes going wide as my fingers curl against my palms. "You've got to be kidding me. What are you *doing*?"

"We're not done," he hisses, so close to my face that I can feel his warm breath on my skin. He whirls me around, dragging me further behind the building so that we're not visible through the window to the two women inside. "You thought it was so cute, didn't you? To sit in there and make a fucking mockery of me?"

His voice rises as he talks, hands on my sleeves trembling. I take it all in calmly, though some part of me stirs with the fear that he's going to hurt me.

Maybe I'm not afraid of him, but apparently he doesn't know that. My body isn't so sure anymore, either, though I refuse to let myself fall into a pit of fear.

After all, he's nothing compared to Gabriel. He's nothing

compared to the man who walks in my dreams and nightmares alike. Nothing like the man who'd followed me all the way from Springwood.

Compared to him, this is just an unfortunate interruption to my day.

"As I told you before, Mr. Durham," I say, stepping closer as I try to ignore the pain of his tight grip. "I can't do my *fucking job* if you yell at me. And if you assault me, I'll have to report it to the police. You think your chances of custody are bad now? Assault your fucking social worker. See how far you can throw yourself down the drain."

It doesn't dawn on me until I suck in a breath and smell the alcohol seeping from his pores, that reason is out the window. His eyes flit round my face, and it occurs to me he might not know what I'm saying, or see the logic behind it. But unfortunately, I'm not good with drunks. I never have been, and I don't think I'm about to start now.

"You need to *listen*," he snarls for the third time since he'd walked into my office. "Just, just *listen,* and—"

I belatedly register the look on his face, and the way his expression contorts to something like fear. I barely notice the shadow that falls over me, just as a body forces itself between Mr. Durham and me. I'm shoved backward, and for just a moment I see his face as he's shoved hard back into the wall that he'd been trying to drag me to.

"The way I see it, you've made a mistake." Gabriel's voice is smooth, dangerous, and sends shudders down my spine. "Make another, and you're going to regret it before the sun sets."

Fuck. My body seems to light up, nerve endings suddenly on fire. "I'm fine," I tell him, my voice soft. "I didn't need your help, Gabriel."

He ignores me, though I'm not shocked. Gabriel leans close

to Mr. Durham, whispering a threat that I'm sure I could guess at but can't hear. Part of me wishes I could, and I feel as if I'm vibrating in place; my teeth sunk into my bottom lip to steady myself.

There's a tense moment where Mr. Durham watches Gabriel, eyes wide... But it doesn't last. It can't when Gabriel is such an unstoppable storm and Durham is just a terrified stop sign ready to be ripped out of the ground.

He bolts, not looking back, until he's out of sight around the cars. I watch, trying to see where he goes, but it's impossible to see once he's disappeared down the street and I can't see him past the parking lot next to ours.

Once he's gone, my hands flex, skin clammy as I try to figure out what to say to the man still here, who's looking at me like he wants me to speak.

"Why would you do that?" I ask finally, my voice quiet. "Because you think I can't take care of *myself*?"

Gabriel chuckles and turns to face me with his hands shoved into his pockets. "Not at all, sweet girl," he says, taking a step closer to me so he's invading my personal space. "You could've killed him, couldn't you? I bet you could've made him sorry. But just this once, I couldn't help myself, Quinn. I needed to remind myself of it, you know?"

My blood runs cold, and I scrub my hands on my jeans to dry them. "Of what?" I ask, my voice soft and reluctant.

"Of the fact that you're mine, obviously."

CHAPTER
ELEVEN

his is the moment that I run.

We both know it, and the fear spiking in my body is a testament to how much we know it. This is the point where I flee to my car, or back inside if I'm too scared of being alone with him for a second longer. He's said those magic words that send me into fight-or-flight. He isn't cornering me, but he might as well be.

This is definitely the moment that I flee... but today, something changes. The pointer picks the other box instead, and before I know what I'm doing, I stride forward with a snarl and *shove* Gabriel Brooks hard in the chest, as if he's going anywhere.

Miraculously, he takes a step back. The confusion on his face is the same as what I feel, and my breath comes in angry gasps as I crowd him in the parking lot, further from the building.

"How *dare* you?" I hiss, hoping that I sound threatening. There isn't a hint of fear on his face, and the mix of intrigue and amusement almost makes me hesitate.

But not quite.

"I never asked for your help, and I am not *yours*." I shove him again and he steps back one more time until we're between two SUVs in the parking lot and completely blocked from curious eyes.

That should make me pause, but it doesn't either. It doesn't do more than blow past my thoughts, and it's not even a factor in my decision-making. "You were my *therapist*, not whatever else you think you were."

This time, when I reach up to shove him, he catches my arms and swings me hard into the black SUV at my back. It's a wonder the alarm doesn't go off, though the model looks old enough that maybe it doesn't have a working security system.

"I was wondering when this side of you would come out to play. You look like you could stab me, Quinn. With all that anger and righteous indignation. Tell me, does it hurt?"

"Does *what* hurt?" I hiss, trying to push him away.

But this time, he doesn't move.

"Sitting on that fucking high horse of yours all the time. Let me drag you down and give you a little break from being better than me. How does that sound?" When I move again, his hand shoots out to press against my throat, fingers wrapping around my neck as his body presses to mine.

"I'm not—" I begin, but he cuts off my air and I can't help but choke.

"Better than me? Maybe you are, just a little. But not because of your personality. It was merely an opportunity. Maybe I should've let it go. I should've let him drag you into the bushes." My stomach flips, and when I suck in a breath, the cold feeling of fear works its way up my spine.

"That's fucked up," I whisper, and it's like Gabriel is leeching the heat from me. He crowds me, his height and muscle more imposing than I could ever be, and when he slides his knee in between my thighs, it radiates heat against my body.

"Why? *Why*, Quinn? Is it fucked up because in your mind you're convincing yourself that I want something bad to happen to you?" He lunges forward, teeth coming together centimeters from my lips so he can grin broadly at me. "Or is it fucked up to let you do all the nasty little things that I know you were thinking of?"

The bottom drops out from my stomach, and I feel like the ground yawns open under me. Flickers from the diner, from the past, try to overwhelm my brain, but I shake my head to chase them and his voice away. "You don't know what you're talking about. I'm not what you *think*," I hiss. "I'm not *like you*."

"You want to be," he accuses. "Isn't that what you're so afraid of?" His mouth is still too close, much too close, and when my lips part so I can argue, he makes his move.

Gabriel's lips find mine in a bruising kiss, and as if to pay me back from a few nights ago, he wastes no time in biting down *hard*.

I cry out in pain, the harsh, sharp burn bolting down my body as my mouth opens wider. He drinks in the sound as he laps the blood from my lower lip, and it takes me seconds to realize that his knee against my body is rubbing against me, sending undeniable friction through my core.

"Stop," I tell him, heart pounding as I reach up to try to do what he does to me. My fingers aren't long enough to curl around his throat like he does around mine, but I copy his movements anyway and slide my finger and thumb just under the stubble of his jaw.

"You want to play like this? Do you want to see who can *last*, Quinn?" There's something in his eyes that sends my pulse skyrocketing, and I wonder if he can feel it in the pads of his fingers. "Let me help you." He reaches up with his free hand to adjust my hand, putting it in a better place so my thumb and forefinger can sink into his skin more comfortably. "Now you just press. Just *press*, Quinn." His words are an order, and the hesitation vanishes as I follow it. I press hard, and he does the same.

In fact, he mirrors every movement I make. When my grip lightens, his does too, so when I push even harder against his pulse, he does as well, and I see stars.

"Right there, baby girl," he grates out, leaning forward again and forcing my thighs wide against his knee. "You'll have to do better if you want to hurt me, though. Come on. Press harder."

I do.

I'm not expecting the wave of heat that goes through me when he mimics the pressure, and I choke for air as my vision blurs and goes double.

"Don't give up on me now," he urges, still moving against me. "I know you have more fight in you than this."

"Stop," I gasp, my hand slipping from his neck to grip the collar of his shirt instead. "*Stop,* I ca-I can't—"

"Let go and just stop fighting me," he urges, able to press against me now that I'm not holding my arm up to his throat. "I've got you. *I've got you, Quinn.* Just like I always have."

"*Please.* You're... you're hurting—"

"You're loving every second of it, my precious little thing," he purrs against my ear. "And you're so desperate for me. Let go, Quinn. Just enjoy it."

"You're—"

"I know how to take care of you." The words echo in my ears just as my fingers release his shirt. I can't help but fall back against the car, and I barely feel his teeth against the base of my throat as my head spins, mind blurring until—

The moment he lets go, I take a gasp of air, and my eyes fly open. My lips part just for him to kiss me again, and his hand on my hips grip so hard I worry that he's leaving bruises.

"*Gabriel*," I hiss, the sound too close to a whimper for me to feel good about it. "Please, please—"

"I know, precious girl, I know. Not here, though. What if someone saw, hmm? What if someone saw you riding my thigh like this, or the way you're begging for me to touch you?"

The humiliation stings as he goads me on, though it doesn't help bring me back to my senses. If anything, it does the exact opposite.

When he kisses me again and worries at the bite in my lower lip, I really do whimper. He urges my arms up and over his shoulders, and forces me higher against the SUV so my weight is resting mostly on his leg.

"One more," he purrs, and I'm not sure if he's promising himself or me. "One more, then I'm leaving. I don't like other people seeing you like this. It's for me, not them." His hand comes up to brush my hair back from my face, and I feel the tremble that works through my body when his thumb presses against my bottom lip.

"Open your mouth," Gabriel orders in a low growl, his eyes bright. "Open your fucking mouth, Quinn."

"I'll bite you," I promise, meeting his gaze with mine. "I'll fucking *bite you*, Gabriel." He doesn't listen, if he hears my breathy words at all. His thumb slips into my mouth, pressing against my tongue, and I do just what I'd told him I would.

I bite him.

My teeth sink into his skin as he whispers a curse against my hair, and his other hand fists in my shirt as a warning as he lets out a soft *fuck* just loudly enough for me to hear.

"Let go," Gabriel orders, fingers twisting my shirt more harshly. "Let go, Quinn. This isn't the place to play like you want."

Like *I* want?

I let go, only to nip at him lightly as his thumb leaves my mouth, just to prove to him that I'm not his to order around.

He smirks, eyes bright, and slams me back against the SUV again, his mouth finding mine so he can kiss me like this is the last chance he'll ever get.

I moan against him, and when he pulls away and drops me to the ground, it's my turn to gasp out a soft string of swears.

Gabriel laughs and sweeps his hair back from his face. "You're such a little monster when you want to be." I can't tell if it's a compliment, so I don't respond. Really, I don't know how to, so I just glare at him. "I'll see you later, Quinn. And I hope you're looking forward to all the things I'm going to do to every *inch* of you the moment I get the chance."

"As if I want you to?" It's a weak argument, and he only stares at me like I'm being an idiot. There's disbelief in his face, and it prompts me to roll my eyes and look away. "Go *away*. Unless you want me to scream about how little I want your help. Again."

"Just so your boss sees us?" he taunts, hands in his pockets. "Maybe not a good idea, since you'll have to explain why we were nearly fucking against her car."

I jerk forward, away from the vehicle, shaking my head. "We were not—"

"Have a good day, Quinn," Gabriel interrupts, chuckling. "Dream of me, won't you?" He doesn't respond to my rude reply, and seconds later, his car is speeding out of the parking lot. Leaving me a confused, anxious mess as I try to pull myself together and figure out what I'm going to do with myself.

CHAPTER

TWELVE

Barely a day later, when I'm back in my cubicle and wishing I'd become something with more pizazz, like a circus clown, I can't get him out of my head.

My neck aches when I turn just right, and I'd been right about his fingers leaving bruises on my hips.

They had, and they look like I've been claimed by a man who had just fucked me, even though Gabriel definitely is not that man.

Nor will he ever be, if only I can get certain parts of me to fall in line.

I close my eyes and rub my palms against them, sighing through my nose and wishing the week would get the hell over with. *It's Friday,* I remind myself. *It's Friday, and you're fine.*

Getting through today means a weekend to sleep, eat cookie dough, and *not* attend Melinda's pool party.

The bolts of colors behind my eyes as I dig my palms against them don't help, however, when every single one of them is either the color of Gabriel's hair or the sparkling brown of his eyes. *Damn it.* Getting myself under control is the first, second, and third step to successfully figuring out how to get him the fuck away from me.

The fourth step is getting the damn tracker out of my car, if it really exists. I'd dedicated a few hours to looking, found nothing, then spent the rest of the day trying to look up what they look like only to find that there are a thousand or so different kinds.

The day had been a bust, all things considered. And I was still no closer to finding out if there really is one hidden somewhere in my car.

There has to be, I reason, my frown dragging my mouth downward. *There's no other way he could keep finding me, unless he's secretly telepathic.* Likely, I suppose, since he somehow seems to know everything I'll enjoy, even when the idea of it makes me squirm.

Like being choked within an inch of consciousness.

My body tingles as I try to shove away the memory. Now isn't the time to think about it. But then, neither was last night, in bed, with my fingers buried between my thighs and my fingers around my own throat.

It had been fucked up in every way, but I'd never gotten off harder in my life.

When a folder slams down in front of me, I jump and look up, blinking hard, to see Clara looking down at me with a clouded expression. Her hand still on the folder tap's it, and she says nothing for a few moments.

She just looks at me.

She saw, I think, already trying to figure out what to tell her. How do I explain what had happened yesterday when I can barely wrap my mind around it myself? "Clara—" I begin, but she cuts me off with what I expect to be irritated jealousy, if not outright hostility. After all, the entire office knows about

Clara's crush on Gabriel. Which is to say, Melinda, Clara, me, and the janitor know.

"I hate to do this to you," she says, lifting her hand off the folder. "Melinda isn't here, but she just called. Can you do something for us? This is one of her cases, but she's thinking maybe you could handle today's job."

I blink down at the folder, not recognizing the name. "What do you need?" I ask slowly, still half-afraid that this is some trick, and she's gearing up to exile me from the island or throw me off the roof.

"The Weathers family needs you to come pick up one of their kids. She can't stay there, but we have another home lined up for her and everything. You just need to pick her up and take her to meet Melinda. She'll be ready to go when you get there. And Melinda will be waiting for you at the McDonalds near the intersection." As there aren't many McDonalds or many intersections in town, I know which one she means. "I would, but I have a meeting. Can you pick her up?"

"Yeah, okay." I get up and pick up the folder, skimming through it, until I find the girl's name and current address.

Lily Jenkins.

My heart twists unexpectedly, and I frown. I've wanted to do this all my life, and this is a bad time to get cold feet.

"Hey, umm. By the way, the Birkin family. Did you hear what happened? Who did it, or...?" I trail off as Clara shakes her head.

"Last I heard from Ed, they're starting to think they did it to each other. But there's nothing official, yet," she explains, naming her cop friend that I'm pretty sure she's sleeping with. "Have a safe trip, okay?"

"Oh. Yeah, umm." I nod at the folder. "Yeah, no problem." My steps carry me out of the office, and thankfully I don't ask any other stupid questions that might doubt her faith in my ability to do this, even though I'm questioning that myself.

"This is your job," I tell myself. "Your job you get paid to do. You're going to help, so it'll be fine. Just don't think too much about it, Quinn." Once I'm in my car, I pull my hair up into a ponytail and sit back, eyes closed.

Of all the days to do this, I never would've preferred today.

Sweat rolls down my face as I stand at the sidewalk and stare at the black garbage bags at my feet. They haven't been allowed for a while now, but what am I supposed to do when the little girl walked out with her belongings in them and tossed them down in front of me?

She'd disappeared back inside, dejected and hollow-eyed, and I still can't figure out how to confront the woman standing on the porch smoking a cigarette that's short enough to scorch her fingers if she moves wrong.

God, I wish she'd move wrong.

The little girl, Lily, comes back out with another bag and drops it, head down, before letting out a long breath. I can't figure out why her foster mother couldn't have helped her, but that's not my only problem right now.

My bigger problem is the fact that this brings back memories I like to avoid. I close my eyes hard and push back the memories of my own belongings in garbage bags and my foster siblings watching from the window as I'm shepherded into another social worker's car.

It *sucked*.

Kneeling down so I'm in front of Lily, I wait for her to look up at me before I smile. "Is this everything? You didn't leave anything by accident?"

The girl hesitates and looks back at her foster mom, who plasters a sour smile on her face and waves.

"She won't let me take my stuffed rabbit," the girl says finally.

"Why not?"

"She says I wasn't a good enough girl to bring it with me."

Anger churns my stomach as I stand and pop the trunk of my car. The bags are light enough that it only takes me one trip to get them, and by the time Lily is in my back seat with the AC on blast and a water bottle in hand, I'm ready to explode. Tremors make me clench my hands, and I turn on my heel to march toward the stairs.

"Did you need me to sign something else?" the woman asks lazily, rubbing her cigarette out on the porch railing. "Melinda already—"

"I need Lily's stuffed rabbit," I interrupt, not bothering to stop at the bottom of the stairs politely. "Where is it?"

The woman looks at me, dumbfounded, before glancing from side to side. "What rabbit?" she asks finally. "If there's a rabbit, it's in—"

"It's in your house," I say, finding myself sure that Lily isn't lying or mistaken. "If you want, I can go look for it. Or you can bring it to me instead. I don't mind either way."

She meets my gaze with her pale blue eyes. I can't help but wonder if age and nicotine have leeched the color from them, rendering them more grey than blue, but I don't look away. Not even when the scent of smoke curls my insides, my nose burning from it.

"I'll go get it for you," she snaps finally, flicking the butt of her cigarette in my direction. I don't follow her as she turns on her heels, though I give her a mental count of fifty before I break down the door and go get it myself.

If this woman thinks that just because I'm young, I'm willing to let her walk all over me, she'll be sorely disappointed.

Thankfully, it only takes her until forty-two to come out, and she thrusts a stuffed rabbit into my arms that's half-missing an ear. I take it gingerly, treating it like it's alive and not just a worn out toy. "You're new," she observes, looking me over coldly. "You'll let these kids walk all over you if you don't grow a damn backbone."

As she says it, I examine the rabbit and run my fingers along the soft but worn fur. "I'm new," I agree, my eyes flicking up to hers. I feel cold, and with the cold comes the absence of anything except irritation and immense dislike of the woman for how she's treating this girl. "But I'm not letting anyone walk all over me. And trust me, I'm pretty experienced in the foster care industry, *ma'am*." She holds my gaze for a moment more before turning and going back inside, slamming the door in my face.

It's for the better, I think, as I jog back to my car and present the little brown-haired girl with her rabbit. A smile touches her lips, though it's wary at best as she pulls the toy to her chest and hugs it hard.

I was that little girl once, and seeing her like this, so hopeful and yet also so scared for what's to come, *hurts*.

"Do you like milkshakes?" I ask, pulling the car out onto the empty suburban street.

"I like chocolate milkshakes," Lily replies after a few moments to think it over. "Are you getting me a milkshake so you can tell me something bad? You don't have to. I know how this works."

"Uh, heck no," I tell her, grinning in the mirror so she can see me in the back seat. "I'm getting you a milkshake and fries so we can wait for Melinda in style and not sweat our butts off. I'm not from here," I add, trying to make conversation. "Is it always so hot? It's only June!"

The little girl's smile widens at my own over the top attitude. "It's summer!" she replies, like she's the adult and I'm the clueless child. "Of course it's hot."

"Milkshake hot," I say, and pull into the first fast food place that I find to get both of us fries, milkshakes, and chicken nuggets.

"For if she's late," I say, when Lily questions this too. "Besides, everyone needs chicken nuggets."

It isn't until Lily is in Melinda's car, extra-large milkshake not even half empty, that I stop to take a breath. I know how I must look, and I'm sure Melinda isn't fooled.

Especially when she comes to stand in front of me, her figure blocking Lily from my gaze as she rests a hand on my shoulder. "The first one is always hard," she says, her own voice soft. "The hardest, until you see something so terrible you dream about it. We live in a poorer area, and parents here struggle."

"She shouldn't have trash bags," I say, the words like sharp-edged blades in my mouth. "That's not right. They aren't allowed anymore, and—"

"I know." She squeezes my shoulder and I look up into her face. "We're going to have a chat with her ex-foster mom. We're going to make sure she knows that isn't acceptable from here on out."

"What did she do, anyway?" I ask, knowing most kids get moved because a home isn't quite right, or they act out. "Did she hurt someone?"

Melinda is quiet for a few moments, and I blink up at her face as she goes through her thoughts. "She's a good kid," my boss says finally. "And she wasn't the problem in that house."

"She wasn't? Then—"

"Their teenage son was."

The words nearly knock me over, and Melinda's hand tightening on my shoulder is the thing I hold onto. My eyes close hard, and I fight not to cry as my heart breaks into pieces for the little girl in the car who I'd bought a milkshake for only a few minutes ago.

"Will she be okay?" I ask, forcing myself to open my eyes and not say anything worse. "She's going to another foster home, right?"

"A *great* foster home," my boss promises. "I pulled some strings and she's going to one of the best homes I have. We'll be investigating her last home, too. It's not just the trash bags, as you now know. There are two boys there; I'll be looking to get them out as soon as possible."

The words make me feel better, but only a little. It isn't enough.

The mother and her teenage son deserve more. They deserve worse than a fucking reprimand and their payment from the government cut. But I know that my words aren't going to do anything, so I just nod and stare at the air over her shoulder.

"Have you thought about seeing a therapist?" Melinda asks, and I nearly scoff at the irony. From foster kid to social worker, it seems I'll never escape the need for a therapist in this life. "Most of us do. All of us do, actually. From one time to another. Evaluations help all of us do our job, and it's something I recommend for my workers. Especially when there are so few of us and we're stretched so thin. I want you to see someone."

"I'll... look around," I agree, only half listening to her. "I'll ask Clara who she sees, or—"

"I think you should see Dr. Brooks," Melinda states, cutting me off. "He's signed a contract with the office, and has made himself available for the social workers at no charge. He seems like a great guy, Quinn." Her comforting squeeze on my shoulder suddenly feels like a threat, though I can't move.

If I say anything, I'll say the wrong thing.

I'll let on that I know him. I'll let on *what he is.*

I can't do that. Not here.

"No, I umm..." She won't accept no for an answer. I get that. So I jerk my head in a nod, and give her a smile that I force onto my lips. "Okay," I lie, knowing I won't do anything I say I will when it comes to him. "I'll get his number from the office. I'll see if he has an opening."

"I can call, if you'd rather," she offers, her words kind. "I don't mind."

Already I'm shaking my head. "No, Melinda. It's okay. I'd prefer to handle it myself, actually." Though in this case what I'm really trying to say is that I won't be handling it at all.

He isn't my therapist anymore, and I'll go back to him over my dead and very cold body.

CHAPTER
THIRTEEN

S omething isn't right.

Well, apart from me standing outside of the house where the Birkin couple were murdered, leaving their kids permanently in foster care, leaning on my car, and skimming my eyes over their file from the folder in Melinda's office. I was smart, I'd made copies, and now I'm looking at papers that are mine and mine alone.

Something isn't right, and even though I'm not from here, I can tell. The police tape is gone. There's nothing here that even looks like it was a crime scene barely a week and a half ago. Hell, there's even a for sale sign and the yard has been cleaned up.

As if everyone is trying to move on and pretend it never happened. But that isn't right, is it? When there hasn't been conclusive evidence on who in the world killed the Birkins?

I let out a breath as my phone rings, the number familiar enough that I frown. Though, I only know it's Gabriel because of his card. I've certainly never picked up the phone to call him. Not that I ever would, either.

"What?" I ask, voice dry as I hold the phone to my ear. "What do you want?"

"*You.*" The word is simple, to the point, and makes my heart thud nervously in my chest. My teeth press against my lower lip, sinking into it until my eyes water and I feel collected enough to take a breath.

"Well that's not happening, so what else do you want?"

"*No, I mean you're supposed to be here today.*" He sounds so patient, like I'm a disorderly child he's talking to instead of an adult with a social work degree. "*Melinda made you an appointment, and she said you'd signed off on it. Where are you, Quinn?*"

"Not there," I reply lightly. "I'm not going to you for therapy, Gabriel." I sound braver than I am, and I pause when he chuckles.

"*Why? I'm the best therapist you've ever had. Do you think I can't help you now just like I helped you back then? Or are you afraid I'll help more than you want me to?*" There's some kind of challenge in his voice, like he's trying to taunt me into action.

But I'm not angry today, and he's not going to push me that far.

"Actually there's this really nice lady in Eddyville I'm going to go see instead. She works with adults that have PTSD, and has a great report with social workers," I inform him sweetly. "She seems a lot more like what I need. But you understand, right? After all, you were the one who told me that it was all about finding the right therapist."

"*Yeah. And your right therapist is me.*" There's a note of something in his voice that I can't place. Something that goes past the usual cruel, yet playful nature he exudes. "*Careful with the mistakes you make, darling. One day you might regret the consequences.*"

There's silence between us, and I try not to think of all the ways he's right about being my therapist. He really is the best I've ever had, though I'm determined not to say those words out loud when he's on the phone with me. I can't do this. I can't do this with *him*, more specifically. I can't let him in like I had before. After all, who's to say he won't kill me if I disappoint him?

"I'm hanging up now," I say, closing the folder in my hands. "I don't have time for this today."

"*Do what you want.*" The sudden shift gives me pause, and I glance up at the house with narrowed eyes.

"Oh yeah?"

"*Yes. Do what you want, Quinn. It's a free country after all.*" His tone doesn't match the words, sure, but I'm not about to question it.

"Whatever, then," I reply, sniffing with disdain. "Sorry to mess up your therapy schedule, or whatever. But hey, call Clara, won't you? I'm sure she—"

He hangs up, the phone going dead in my ear, and I snort. With a shake of my head I toss the folder back into my car, but before I can walk around to the driver's side, I give the house another look.

I want to see what's inside, because of some fucked up, macabre curiosity that can't be tamed in my chest. Besides, with this not being a crime scene anymore, who cares? No one is likely to stop me. Unless the realtor shows up. But I doubt that's going to happen.

Paducah is a small enough town that there isn't much happening here this late in the day. Even on a Friday. I can do whatever I want here, and I won't get caught. Hell, no one would even know to come looking for me here. It's the perfect situation for exploring places I shouldn't be.

My walk to the house is just as it had been before, and the steps are still a tetanus trap of loose nails. The railing is still bad as well, so it seems that any clean up or fixing up that had been done here were superficial at best.

The door handle turns under my grip and I walk in, my eyes on the kitchen that I'd been in before. Today there's... nothing. No blood, no bodies, nothing to make it look like anything had happened here whatsoever.

But still I take a moment, exploring the kitchen and bending down to look at things even though there's nothing to see, before moving on to the living room. It's nicer and cleaner than I expect too, shining for all its cheapness, and I breeze by it until I find the main bedroom that sits on the first floor.

Or rather, what I *think* is the main bedroom. It looks like a primary suite, with a bathroom and closet with a worn and rickety door nearly hanging from its hinges. For all of that, however, there's nothing. No furniture. No bed. Just... *nothing*. I travel to the bathroom next, and search the clean cabinets for anything of note.

Nothing except the smell of bleach. Whoever cleaned this place had done so extra thoroughly, but I don't understand why. Especially when it's the main bed- and bathroom, instead of the other rooms that I've seen. Even the kitchen isn't as clean, isn't as *perfect* as this strangely empty room.

But if there's something to hide here, wouldn't it have been in the kitchen where the Birkins were killed? Wouldn't that be the place to bleach within an inch of its life, instead of coming in here and doing it?

Quickly I look through the rest of the house, which is intact and as clean as it can be, before coming back to the strange not-bedroom and looking through it one more time. Something feels off, like a clue just beneath the fresh paint on the walls, but short of scraping it off, I don't know what I'm going to do.

Hell, I don't even know what there *is* to do. Especially since the cops have cleared it and there's nothing here except new paint and bad memories.

The thought irritates me as I leave, and I barely look back at the house as I all but jog to my car. It's creepy here, and things just feel strange to me, like I'm being watched. The sooner I'm gone, the better, even if I don't understand the itchy, uncomfortable feeling being here brings.

The file is in my passenger seat where I left it as I get into my driver's seat, and I take a moment to lean back against my seat, eyes closed, and just *breathe.*

I need to get myself together. If I'm going to handle any of this the right way and not lose my sense over the dumbest thing, then I need to just—

The hand over my mouth jerks me back hard and I shriek, thrashing in the driver's seat, only to be trapped by the seat belt I'd already buckled. Another hand wraps around my throat, keeping me in place, and my eyes snap open as I try to see who's behind me.

They don't make any sound, however. Instead, they shift their hand until the rag they're holding covers my mouth and nose more profoundly, and with horror I can feel the dizziness in my head increasing, causing my limbs to feel heavier with every thrash.

"No!" I scream, trying to lunge forward and only succeed in hurting myself with the seat belt. "*No!*" I shriek again, my arm slamming against the horn over and over, for anyone to hear me, even as my struggles wane.

I realize as my head falls back against the seat and my breaths deepen against my will. Who's going to hear me when I timed my visit so perfectly for no one to know where I was? Who's going to save me when there's no one around except the ghosts of the Birkins and the person in my backseat who refuses to say a word?

FOURTEEN

I t's the sound of the AC kicking on that makes me realize I'm waking up.

I groan softly and curl further into myself, the pillow under my face soft against my cheek. Is it Saturday? I don't remember going to sleep, but I also don't remember what I did after going to the weird murder house.

Had I gone in?

Slowly my memories ebb back, of talking to Gabriel and refusing his therapy. Of the pristine kitchen and empty bedroom, and the rest of the house that had been as boring as could be.

With it being Friday, I'd hoped to come home, eat tacos, and make milkshakes. Since it's my Friday ritual, I try to be home by eight, so I'm not eating at two in the morning.

But I don't remember any of that. Though, unless I've fallen asleep on the couch, it had to have happened.

My brain searches for the lost memories as I slowly wake up more. My fingers flex and I rub my nose into the softness of the couch behind me. Maybe it's still night, I think, and I'm about to burn the house down with tacos on the stove or a blender full of ice cream that's about to explode.

But I don't even remember going home.

Finally, something pulls my attention to one thought, one sliver of a memory. It starts with discomfort, and a cloth pressed to my nose and mouth. I'd breathed in deep and deeper, feeling my body relax against my will.

Had that really happened?

"Are you in pain at all?" The voice rockets me back to when I'd been a teenager and Gabriel had been so good at making me think he was the man he pretended to be. It's his therapist voice that I haven't heard in a long time, and my eyes fly open as I sit up fast.

Immediately I regret it, however. I groan and fall back onto my elbows, eyes squeezed shut as the world spins and dips around me.

"What did you do to me?" I moan, wondering if I'm going to throw up. "Why do I feel like this?"

"You made it easy," Gabriel replies kindly. "But then, you're always so good at being predictable for me, aren't you?" I hate the way he says it, but I find I can't disagree at the moment. "I knocked you out. You'll be fine, especially when you get up and start moving around to clear your head."

He moves, though I only know by the way it sounds when he walks across the room. I can't help but flinch when he touches me, and my eyes open again to fix on his face that swims into focus. "Let me help you," he says sweetly, gently, and in a way that makes me want to punch him. "Come on, Quinn. Let me help you."

"No," I say blatantly. "No, if you feel bad, you shouldn't have drugged me, knocked me out, dragged me here—"

"Actually," he cuts me off smoothly and kneels beside the couch, his smile turning less friendly. "I never said I was sorry, darling. I only said I'd help you work this off." Before I can stop him, he pulls me into a sitting position, and even though I protest with curses and try to bite his arm, drags me into a standing position.

I can't hold myself up. That much is apparently instantly, and I fall into him with a gasp, worried he's going to drop me.

He doesn't, though.

I suck in air as I clutch him, wishing my head wasn't spinning like a carousel and that I could get my legs under me. My fingers clutch hard at him as he steadies me, holding both of us up and not voicing a word of complaint.

"I hate you," I mutter, just in case he isn't aware of it. "I *hate* you, Gabriel."

"That's something we can talk about. Can you stand up on your own now?" He rests me more steadily on my feet, and when he pulls away, I find that I can. Barely. My hands are still clutched in his v-neck, long-sleeved tee, but that's all. I suck in air, trying to clear my head, and some part of me is grateful that he's not pushing me for more right now.

After all, it's going to be a few minutes before I can break his nose.

"Can you walk a little?" He pulls away, leading me into taking a few steps. I stagger, placing one foot in front of the other, and groan softly to voice my displeasure. I can walk, but I'm not having a great time. In fact, none of this is what I'd consider a good time.

"Fuck," I whisper, taking a few more dizzying steps. I pull away from him finally, walking slowly around the room with my palms pressed to my eyes. "What do you *want*?" I snap when I finally feel like I'm not going to pass out. "You can't just kidnap me, *drug* me, whatever. This is fucked, Gabriel." I turn to glare at him as I say it, taking in the office and the desk he sits at.

It's nice. Nicer than any office would be, and when I look through the French doors behind me, I realize with a jolt that we're in his house.

It's certainly a lot nicer than the one I've rented for myself. Fresh paint, hardwood floors, and tray ceilings meet my eyes, insulting me with their upscale appearance. It's definitely bigger than the house I'm renting as well, and as I peek through the French doors, I catch sight of a large living room with a sofa facing a television mounted over a long, modern-looking fireplace.

"We could go into another room if you want," Gabriel offers lazily from behind his big mahogany desk. It's similar to the one he had in Springwood, and this whole room reminds me of a better version of that office.

"I'd rather just leave," I reply, trying the door handle.

It's locked.

Of course, it's locked, because Gabriel is always so damned good at thinking of everything in all the worst ways. Even if it wasn't, I would've expected him to have traps set outside to keep me in here with him. Unless he's planning on knocking me down and dragging me back in himself, should I escape. Which is always an option.

"Chair or couch, your choice of where you sit. But you *are* sitting, so..." he trails off as I look at him, shrugging his shoulders. "The sooner you get over here, the sooner you can leave. How does that sound?"

He makes a good point, and a better offer. I waver for half a second more before striding over to his side of the room, my head finally clear, and drop myself into the plush armchair in front of his desk to glare at him balefully.

It does no good. He barely seems as if he notices, and

instead pulls out his iPad and stylus, a notes doc already up with my name at the top.

"Seriously? You're doing this for real?" I ask, more surprised than anything else. "I thought this was some stupid excuse to make veiled threats and promises you think turn me on."

"*Do* they turn you on?" he asks, looking down at his notes and scrawling something in his messy hand. I can't read it from this far, especially upside down, but I doubt I'd be thrilled at whatever it says.

"Nope."

"Are you sure? I really felt like that wasn't the case in the parking lot the other day." His hand pauses, long fingers stroking along the edge of the stylus. "Or are we pretending that didn't happen?"

"I'm not talking to you about that. This is about *work*, right? How Melinda is worried about me for no reason." I don't want to talk about us, or him. I don't want to talk to him about anything. Especially when it comes to my job.

But unfortunately, he seems like he isn't willing to accept that as an answer.

Gabriel taps the stylus gently on his desk, eyes dragging up to meet mine. "Are your nightmares happening every night?" he murmurs, making my fingers itch. "Ever since you started taking cases at work?"

"Who cares?"

"Has it occurred to you that being a social worker is dragging up parts of your past that you've been trying to forget?"

His words make my stomach twist and I look away. My eyes land on the book case instead, and I walk over to it to examine the titles.

A History of Bees.

Fun and Fudge in the Kitchen.

If there was any doubt before that this house isn't his, it's gone now. I can't see him reading about bees, fudge, *or* fun. Definitely not fun.

"I don't need your help," I say, turning to look at him and leaning against the heavy wood shelves. Crossing one ankle over the other as I do, praying I'm no longer too woozy to keep my balance. "I haven't needed it in years. Can you please, *please* not do this to me?"

He holds my gaze, sympathy flashing through his caramel eyes. "It's my job," he reminds me sweetly, a smile curling over his full lips. "I'm just trying to help you."

"If you were trying to help me, you'd tell me where the tracker in my car is!" I can't help the way I snap at him, nor can I help the aggressive jerk toward him I can't stop myself from.

"Oh, so we can't find it, can we?" He writes something else down with a flourish. "I'm actually surprised. Have you tried taking your car somewhere? They'll look for it. They'd have an easier time finding it than you, since I doubt you even know what you're looking for."

"I wanted to." I stride over to press my hands against his desk, standing over him. "But it costs *money*. Which is something I'm in short supply of. Feels like an insult. Feels pretty shitty for you to put me in a situation that I financially can't handle right now."

He looks at his notes, writing more words I can't read, even from this distance. Then he lays the stylus down and looks up at me until our faces are too close for comfort and I'm wishing I hadn't come so close.

"Is that supposed to make me feel bad?" he asks lazily, his voice soft. "Am I supposed to... what? Break down and tell you where it is? Tell you what it looks like and offer to take it out for you? Do you really think that's what's going to happen here, Quinn?"

The air is still between us, and his warm breath is the only spot of heat on my skin as goosebumps break out over my arms and a tingle goes down my spine.

"I hate you," I whisper, my temper rising. "You're such an —" I lunge for his stylus, intent on breaking it or at least throwing it out the window. It's childish, it's rash, and above all, it's stupid. But he has a tendency of pushing me too far, to the point where he gets to watch me act like I have no sense.

In fact, I think he enjoys it.

But this time he doesn't just watch. His hand snaps out, pinning my arm down and then using it to yank me down over his desk until I'm flush against it.

"You're very hostile for someone who could use someone to talk to," he whispers in my ear, standing up but keeping his grip on me so I can't. "This isn't how I wanted this to go, Quinn. Why can't you keep a hold of your temper for once?"

My cheeks burn at his chastisement. He's right, and I hate that he makes me so irrationally angry, or worse. He moves until he's pinning me down with a hand at the back of my throat and standing beside his desk, unmoving.

I writhe, squirming enough to send some of his desk things to the floor. Still, he doesn't move; finally I'm forced to give up my efforts with a frustrated snarl and try to kick out at him in irritation.

Naturally, I miss.

"What are you doing?!" I snap at last, groping around with my hand in an attempt to find his wrist. My face flushes, hot with embarrassment and frustration as my heart pounds. I want him to let go. To get off of me and hopefully fall through the glass door. "Let *go* of me!"

"No," He says simply, moving around the desk so he's behind me. With one leg, he kicks mine apart, sliding his thigh between them before I can regain my balance.

Taking a sharp breath, I try again to move, needing to be more balanced on my feet to do anything other than squirm around like this. But he has me trapped, and with him in between my legs, I can't do more than this.

What's worse is that every time I squirm, every time I move up and down on his desk to try to get away from him, all I feel is the heat and pressure of his thigh against my body. Through the thin material of my shorts, it feels like I'm intentionally grinding along his thigh. The thought makes more embarrassment burn through my veins. It's a combination of that and irritation that I finally stop, my cheek on his desk, and close my eyes hard as I pant out my frustration.

"Can you let me up?" I ask, trying to make it sound like a request and not an order. "*Please?*"

"I could," Gabriel replies, moving so he can press his thigh more forcefully against me. "But you were having such a good time. What's wrong, baby girl? Was it too much for you?" He slides it against me, doing a much better job of hitting all the right places than I had.

"Can you *not?*" I snap, trying and failing once more to wiggle free. "I'll do your stupid therapy, all right? Just let me up."

"I think we'll do it right here. How long have you been having nightmares, Quinn?" he asks offhandedly, surprising me with the frankness of his question.

"Since I was six," I snap, rolling my eyes. "Which you already knew—" His hand comes down on my thigh, just below the curve of my ass, with a smack that echoes in my ears and stops my words dead in my throat. "What are you—"

"How long since you moved here have you been having nightmares?"

"Since I started taking cases," I reply softly, still stunned.

His hand rubs over the place he'd hit, fingers gentle and teasing.

"Explain to me how they make you feel. Are they all about the bad house? The one with your abusive foster father?"

When I don't answer right away, he taps my thigh in warning. I don't care. I don't need him doing this to me, or dragging up the problems of—

He smacks me again, causing me to writhe against his thigh, once more. "Yes, *yes*," I hiss between clenched teeth, feeling my thighs tremble. "They're always about the bad house and always involving my foster father. It's always the night he broke my arm. Sometimes you're there and you kill him. Sometimes I do and he just keeps getting up. Can you please let me get up now?"

"No." He shoves the material of my shorts higher, and I burn with embarrassment as he grips my thigh in his free hand. "Do you think these cases are doing you any good, Quinn? Is the life you'd always dreamed of?"

No.

I hate the way the silent admission makes me feel, and I close my eyes against the coldness of his desk. His fingers move upward, stroking over my skin, and a soft, almost-sigh leaves him.

"Come on, do your worst. Let's go. Can't be worse than—" I don't get to finish. He does smack my thigh again, lightly, but it has me squirming against him all the same.

"You're so difficult." It sounds like praise when he says it. "You're just so—"

I shove myself upward the moment his hand between my shoulders relaxes. He's too slow to stop me, and I fight until I'm sliding off of his desk and to the floor, turning to glare at him. "Smarter than you today," I reply, voice taunting as I grin.

But he doesn't stop to appreciate my creative, amazing

escape. Gabriel moves to grab me again, and succeeds in gripping my arm. It's not a big deal, not something I can't recover from; until it is. He jerks me toward him, using my momentum to swing me around and slam me against the bookshelf. *Fun and Fudge in the Kitchen* clatters to the floor, nearly followed by a few other books that I hadn't read the titles of.

"Are you?" he asks, pinning my hands above my head with one hand, fingers wrapped around my wrist. I fight him, but he's so much stronger than me it's completely futile, and all I get is a pounding heart and my lungs gasping for air. "Are you so much smarter than me, darling?" He shoves his knee between my thighs again, forcing them apart.

"What are you doing?" I hiss, hating that he has one hand free to do whatever he wants with.

His grin is quick, and not at all friendly. "Whatever the fuck I want, Quinn. And you'll enjoy every second of it." He doesn't give me the chance to argue. His free hand grips my shirt, twisting it until my stomach is exposed. He leans forward, catching my bottom lip sharply between his and biting down until I cry out at the burning, throbbing pain.

Only when I'm sure he's drawn blood does he move, turning the bite into a full-blown, filthy kiss with his mouth pressed so hard to mine that I can barely move, let alone do anything except enjoy it. Still, I protest, the sounds swallowed eagerly by him as he kisses me, thigh moving against my body.

"I don't know who you think you're fooling," he murmurs, the moment he pulls away and I'm still panting from his kiss. "Because it certainly isn't me."

"I don't know what you mean," I whisper, never breaking eye contact. "I'm not—"

"Fooling anyone," he agrees, shoving me back against the bookcase again. "So when I shove my fingers into you, your

109

cunt won't be wet for me? You weren't getting off on getting spanked by me during therapy?"

I shake my head, hating that he might be right. I can feel how hot I am, how every time he rubs against me, bolts of electricity shoot up my spine.

"If I'm wet, it's not for you," I promise, my voice only slightly shaking.

"Then what's it for, darling girl?"

"The violence."

It's a weak excuse. A terrible one that I can't even bother to explain. Gabriel stares at me, as if in shock, before a wide grin curls over his features. "I could see that," he laughs finally. "Maybe. Are you admitting to being wet, then? To getting off on this?"

"No."

He doesn't answer. He doesn't need to, when the hand he uses to drag my shorts far enough down and slide his fingers between my thighs is answer enough. I suck in a gasp, mouth open in a protest, only for his lips to find mine again in another punishing, bruising kiss.

But it doesn't distract me from his hand. His fingers rub against my slit through my panties twice, then he's pushing them to the side with one finger as two others slide into me. They do so easily, proving just how right he is and dragging a long moan from my mouth that he swallows eagerly.

He thrusts them in and out, mouth never leaving mine as he leisurely fucks me on two fingers, dragging me slowly toward what promises to be an achingly good release.

At least, until he pulls them away, leaving me empty. I whine, hating the sound as it leaves my lips into his mouth, and watch as he pulls away to lift his hand between us.

"Seems like it's from more than just the violence," Gabriel

purrs, showing me his fingers that are coated in my wetness. "But you tell me."

I open my mouth to argue as my stomach flips and twists itself into knots. My body is *begging* for his fingers back, or something better, but before I can say a word, his fingers are at my lips, shoving between them until he can press them against my tongue.

It hits me then that it's not an answer he wants at all. It's to prove a point. As his fingers curl against my tongue, forcing me to taste my own wetness, it's clear on his face that he's enjoying this just as much as me.

"Seems a bit much, don't you think? I'm leaning toward it being from me and the way I touch you." His words are husky, soft, and rough. He wants more than this, pulling his fingers from my lips and wiping them across my face. "Sit with that for a while," he purrs as I open my mouth in complaint. "That's my official 'homework' for you as your therapist."

He steps back and I stumble forward, nearly falling to my knees on the floor. "You can go now," he says, back to all business formal once again. He walks away as I watch, as if we hadn't been up against his bookcase with his fingers inside of me.

Gabriel sits in his chair, looking up when he sees I haven't moved. "Your session's over," he says, as if reminding me. "You can go now, Quinn. I believe you'll find your keys in your car, which is parked in the driveway."

"Fuck you," I hiss, finally managing to stumble towards the door as my cheeks burn. "Fuck you!"

"Maybe next time," he agrees. "But I don't think insurance will pay for that much overtime today." His grin is savage and teasing. Cruel in the sharpness of his face.

There's so much more I want to say. I want to strangle him,

scream at him, and maybe flip over the pretty mahogany desk if I can manage it.

But I don't do any of those things. Instead, I gesture rudely at him, as if that's what I've wanted to do all along, wait for him to unlock the door at his own pace, and try hard not to look like I'm running out of the room as I make the grand escape to my car, where I can scream all I want without anyone to judge or mock me.

CHAPTER

FIFTEEN

When Mr. Durham has the audacity to show up in my office again, I think I'm going to throw something. Most likely my stapler, at his head, but the exact details are still up in the air. At least until I see if he's going to yell or threaten me again.

His eyes find mine, dark in his pinched and tired face, and I lean back in my chair to stare him down, hopefully preventing him from coming over to me.

But of course, life doesn't work like that for me. It would for Gabriel, I'm sure. Especially since he's the one who threw Mr. Durham into a wall, almost through it, and had made him fuck right off. But not me. I'm just the person who *wanted* to chuck him through a glass window and watch him bleed.

He sits down in front of me as I eye him with disdain. My 'therapy session' from two days ago is still too fresh in my mind for me to be anything resembling friendly, and I tap the end of my pen on the table, engaging and disengaging the tip on every smack. If Melinda were here, she'd be disappointed with me. She'd say I was being antisocial and uninviting.

I'd say that's tame for the vibes I'm trying to send Mr. Durham's way. Maybe he's not the source of all of my troubles right now, but he's not exactly going to *soothe* them, either. And I don't feel like being yelled at today.

"What can I help you with, Mr. Durham?" I ask, just as the door opens again and the star of my current bad dreams walks in.

He looks... good. And certainly better than I do today. With his hands shoved into his pockets and his long sleeves shoved up to his elbow, Gabriel is the epitome of aloofness and sexy, bad boy energy. His eternally tousled hair looks perfectly imperfect, and as he takes off his aviators to look around the room, I can't help but notice the way he grins at Clara.

Like she has a chance to be anything other than his victim.

My eyes narrow in surprise, however, when he strides over to her instead of coming toward me as I'd expected. He leans over her desk, mouth curling up at the edges, and says something I can't hear that makes her look down, eyes wide. A small smirk plays at her lips, and I press mine flat, hating the feeling that surges through my chest.

Mr. Durham turns around as well, his brows raised. "I thought the two of you were together," he says in a low voice. "Sure, I figured he was a little old to be your boyfriend. But with the way he acted..." He shrugs his shoulders and turns to look at me instead. "Judgin' by that look on your face, you thought so too."

I switch my attention to the man in front of me, frowning still. "I don't think that. He can be with whoever he wants. I don't care." Still, the tapping of my pen becomes more erratic, and irritation bubbles in my chest. *I don't care,* I remind myself, as if it's even in question.

"Don't mind me givin' you advice, but if you really don't care, you might try acting like it." When he's not screaming, he has a deep southern accent that draws my attention back to him, and I look the man over with surprise.

"You're less mad today," I point out, not caring that it's pretty obvious. "Did you stop drinking, Mr. Durham?"

He shrugs his broad shoulders, still watching me with interest. "Are you this nice all the time, Miss Riley? Or is it just because your boyfriend is flirtin' with your coworker?"

"He's not—"

Clara laughs loudly, the pitch high and fake enough that I know she's trying to impress him. I suck in a breath, letting it out slowly as she continues to giggle and respond to whatever he's said to her.

I need to get a hold of myself. There's no way that I can act like this with him here and able to see me. Besides, this is my job. I can't act like this *at my job.*

"What do you need, Mr. Durham?" I ask again, unsure if he's already answered and I just haven't noticed. "If you're going to ask about your case file, then—"

"I wanted to talk to you about something," he breaks in smoothly. He really is a totally different person than he was the other day. Much more reasonably, conversational, and mostly polite. It's like night and day, and I wonder if anger over losing custody of his child was really all that was spurring him last time. "Not my case file. Melinda called me, so I know how that's going."

I don't say anything as he thinks, though it's clear that he's trying to find the right words for whatever he wants to tell me.

"I saw somethin'," he says at last, dragging his gaze back up to mine. "And since your prince back there is probably making his way over here next, I'd like to discuss it quickly, while blonde and beautiful is holdin' on to his attention like a lifeline." I don't respond to his dramatic analogies, but I do manage to place the now broken pen onto the desk like I haven't spent the last few minutes battering it into oblivion.

"Something like...?" My brows raise as I trail off. "Did you go looking for your daughter, Mr. Durham? If so, you know I have to tell you that—"

"I did not," he denies, shaking his head. "I went to run a delivery by the Birkins' house the other night. It was addressed there, even though I knew they were dead, but I figured I might just take a drive by there anyway. Just to see if anyone was, uh, home for the delivery."

"It's not nice to investigate a crime scene," I say slowly, pointing out the obvious, like I hadn't recently been doing the same thing.

"Too bad it isn't a crime scene anymore. And ain't that the weirdest thing? You know, I'd heard that you were the one who went out there with their letter. Though it's not your case, is it? Mrs. Melinda was workin' on that one with them." He watches me while he says it, as if he's looking for a reaction. If he is, I don't know what it would be. And I don't know what he thinks I know or suspect.

"How did you know that?" I ask after a moment's pause and listening to Clara whisper something to Gabriel. My eyes flick across the room, only to see that Gabriel's full attention is still on the blonde.

So he has the audacity to kidnap me, punish me, and fuck me, but not pay attention to me at the office? The thought rings through my head, souring my thoughts, and I find myself going for the pen once more.

"We were friends." Mr. Durham's voice drags me out of my irritation, and when I look back at him, he glances toward the pair at the far side of the room. "He's sure layin' it on thick, ain't he?"

I just shrug.

"Maybe he's trying to make you jealous. Done anything to piss off your fair doctor back there?"

"No," I snap. "In fact, if someone should be pissed off, it's me. I'm—" I cut myself off and close my eyes hard. "What are we talking about, Mr. Durham? The Birkins? Why?"

"Because there's no real reason only parts of their house is cleaned out like that. And even less reason that the investigation was handled so swiftly, with so little coverage. You know where we are, Miss Riley?" He snorts and sits back hard in his chair. "Only a few hundred miles south of the Ashwick Murders a couple years back. That means, usually, any news of a killing blows up around here."

Squinting, I try to figure out what he's talking about. "The Ashwick murders?" I ask, voice soft. "That sounds familiar, sort of. There was a girl who survived, right? A little girl who saw the killer die in front of her?"

"That's precisely what I'm talking about. Like I said, since then, we get a lot of blowback for being a similar sized town on a lake. Every time someone dies and there's a sniff of foul play, I see three articles asking if the Ashwick Butcher has a copycat in our town. But why not *this* time, hmm?"

I have no idea. And I certainly don't know enough about Ashwick, Indiana, and its murders, to predict the reasoning he might be hinting at. "Okay, so you think it's what, being covered up? Aliens did it, or the government, or—"

"I think someone might know more than what they're lettin' on is all. But who am I to say?" His eyes darken, sadness leeching away at the intensity there. "I'm just a drunk who lost custody of his kid and whose wife left him."

We're quiet for a few moments until Clara's next giggle breaks the silence and I press my face against my hand. "Did you want to discuss your case while you're here?" I ask, finding myself more amenable to the idea than I had been. "We can, if you like."

"Because you want a distraction?" His words aren't particularly unkind, but he's not exactly the epitome of nice.

"Sure," I say, refocusing on him. "According to Melinda, you're doing really well. That's what her notes say, anyway." I gesture to my computer, where I've pulled up his file. "You have a meeting with your counselor on Thursday, right? I think you should continue on the path you've been taking. Seriously, this could work out for you, if—"

"If you give the right impression." The smooth, velvet-like voice wants me to look up at him. So does the imposing shape standing over me. Gabriel leans over my desk and smiles at Mr. Durham. "I'm available to talk as well, if you need something before then. I'm licensed to work with the county, and I'd love to make things better for you, Mr. Durham." While I don't know how he knows the man's name, the alcoholic opposite me squirms in his seat, obviously uncomfortable.

But then again, so am I. I'm just not going to squirm about it. I can't, when he's so close to me and I can feel his scrutiny.

"That's all right." Mr. Durham gets to his feet and dusts off his hands, like he has something on them or is just uncomfortable. I'm willing to bet on the latter, since Gabriel has that effect on people without even trying. "Thanks for your time, Miss Riley. I'll see you soon." He nods at me and turns, walking out of the office without waiting for me to say goodbye.

He also didn't bother to repeat the sentiment to Gabriel.

I sit there, biting my tongue and waiting for the man above me to *move*. "You can go now," I mutter icily. "I didn't need your help." I hate he can make me like this, that he makes me tremble in both fear and anticipation while burning with jealousy at the same time.

"I was worried for you," he murmurs, trailing a hand up my

arm as the door to the staff lounge closes, giving us the room to ourselves.

"Yeah, you really fucking acted like it," I hiss, jerking away from his touch. "Seriously, comrade of the year, right here. I'll put it next to your master therapist award on the shelf you probably have in your room."

"You think I keep trophies?" He moves with me, dragging his fingers up my skin so hard his nails bite lightly into me. I shudder, wishing I hated it, and he does it again. "Well, you're not wrong. But they aren't for being a therapist, or a good boyfriend."

"Good. Because you're not a good therapist, and if you were my boyfriend, you'd *suck* at it," I say, looking anywhere but up at him. "Better be careful, Dr. Brooks. Clara could come back out and see you with me, and then how would you lure her into your bed?"

"I don't want to fuck Clara," Gabriel chuckles. "But I also know what a good relationship with the people around me can offer. Unlike you. Did he upset you, Quinn?"

I shake my head, eyes fixed on my broken pen. He's so close, and caging me in so completely, that I can't move without touching some part of him. Even now, with his hand still on my arm, I don't know where to go or how to escape.

He has me trapped.

"What did he want?"

"He wants to sue you," I lie, not wanting to tell him about what the man had said that has me both nervous and intrigued. "He says he's going to the cops for what you did to him last week. I agreed with him and told him I'd testify against you."

His hand wanders up to curl loosely around my throat, and he pulls me back so my shoulders and head are resting against his stomach. *Fuck.* I take a deep, shuddering breath as his fingers slide easily under my jaw, pressing just enough that I know he's there.

"You get so excited just from my fingers being here," he comments, amusement tinging his voice. "What did he say, Quinn? You're only hiding it because it was something important."

He's right, but I also don't want to repeat the words where anyone might hear me. Melinda could be in her office, and I would never know since she has a door out of the building behind her desk. Clara could come back out at any minute, and I don't think she should overhear either. I hesitate, my hand coming up to rest on his wrist as I think and concentrate of the feeling of his hand around my throat.

"Maybe there's some other time we can talk," I say finally, unsure if this is the right decision. "Maybe you could help me with this case later? I've wanted another pair of eyes on it... Do you think you would have time?"

His thumb strokes my jaw thoughtfully. It's impossible for him not to know what I'm asking, and he hums softly in his chest as if he has to think about the request. "I could make time," he says at last. "How about I go ask Melinda if I can assist you with your case. I'm sure she'll know which one, or be able to find one."

"I'm sure," I agree, kicking myself. I'd meant that we could just talk *later*. Not for him to actually help me with something. But here I am, regretting my words and wishing I'd been clearer.

The door to the staff room opens just as Gabriel steps back and drops his hand. "Yeah, keep me updated," he says, as if we've been having a work conversation. "I'll let you know what I have on my end, Miss Riley." He nods at me and I force a smile to my face, my insides quivering like jelly.

"No problem," I mutter, giving him a false salute that I

know he'll hate. Sure enough, irritation flickers in his brown eyes, and his lips press flat. "I'm at your service, Dr. Brooks." He chuckles, though it's forced at best, and walks over to say something else to Clara before his steps take him toward Melinda's office and out of view.

Clara sits down beside me in my cubicle instead of hers. "What were you two talking about?" she asks, picking up my broken pen and looking at it with confusion. "And what happened to this?"

"Nothing," I lie, and shove a random file at her on my desk. "We were talking about this. I just wanted his opinion."

She opens it, and the picture of Lily stares up at us. *Shit.*

"Oh, I understand." Her frown is kind and caring, soft as she looks at me and studies my face. "It's hard, isn't it? The first kid who's taken from a bad situation?"

"Y-yeah." I wish I'd picked another file. "It's... it's really hard."

"It'll get better." I doubt that, but I watch Clara get to her feet and stretch. "I'll see you tomorrow? My shift's over, and I'd like to get home before the dinner rush hits." There's no dinner rush here, but I'm not about to disagree with whatever reasoning she's making up.

"I'll see you later," I agree, waving and leaning back over my files. "Have a good night, Clara."

She winks at me, like there's a joke I'm missing, and walks to Melinda's office to stick her head in before leaving through the front door, Gabriel behind her and not once looking back at me, though I can't take my eyes off of him until the door closes firmly behind him, cutting off my line of sight.

"Good riddance," I mutter, and shake my head again. "I didn't want you here, anyway." It's a good sentiment. A smart one.

If I only meant it.

CHAPTER
SIXTEEN

No matter how much I tell myself I'm not about to go home and go on some research binge instead of eating ice cream and hibernating, I know it's not the truth. As soon as I've eaten and the dishes are in the dishwasher, I collapse onto the old, threadbare sofa and let out a sigh, eyes closing hard.

Would Gabriel know about Ashwick, if I asked?

I chase the thoughts away like dirt with a broom, and type Ashwick, Indiana, into the search bar to see what pops up.

I'm not disappointed. Article upon article, some citing cults and urban legends while others talking about an actual killer, march down my screen as I scroll through the results. One of them talks about the survivor instead, a girl who was a child at the time of the first murders.

But the more I read, the more I know that this has nothing to do with Ashwick. How could it, when the only similarity is geography? And really, if there were a copycat, wouldn't they be *copycatting*? That doesn't seem to be happening here, when the only dead people had their throats slit, not strange patterns of cuts all over their body.

The last article I read shows me the girl all grown up, and I study Parker Lowell's face for a few moments, noting how tired she looks and how paranoid, before I shake my head and close out of the article. Hopefully she's doing better now, though if it were me, I'm not sure I'd ever be 'better' again.

Finding nothing, I drift back to the top of the page, settling back against the couch as I do. I reach my left hand behind me, and find the bottle of soda on the end table, seated neatly on the coaster. With my other hand, movements slow, I type in Springwood, Illinois, instead.

Police Still Searching for Clawed Killer.

Three Dead, More Suspected.

Formerly Accused Doctor Released From Prison In Light of New Evidence.

I roll my eyes at the last article, clicking it anyway. So it was true. He'd really gotten free because someone else had been found to take the blame, even though Gabriel had done it all along. My fingers drum against my laptop, and I look up at the television. I have no idea what I'm watching, apart from it being food related, and let my attention drift to what appears to be a cooking competition for a few minutes.

Then I type in the name Gabriel Brooks, instead.

Local Psychologist Rewarded for Advancements in Sleep Psychology. I wrinkle my nose at the words of the title, wondering what in the world Gabriel has for people who are still sleeping. Hell, he's made it clear that he thinks it's 'cute' when I sleep. A few more articles talk about his work with lucid dreaming, and I go through them quickly before sitting back and closing my eyes hard.

Has he always been this way? It's hard to remember a lot of what had happened before the incident with the Owens family. It's hard to think about Gabriel before I knew what he was, though there are some things that I can never get out of my head.

The scent of his sharp cologne.

The comfortable couch in his office.

His warm, sweet smile. It's the same he uses on me now, once in a while. And when I think about it, I realize it's one he reserves *just* for me.

Warmth blossoms in my chest, though I fight it back quickly. I shouldn't be happy about him feeling this way about me. I shouldn't be *happy* that his sweetest smiles are for me and me alone. He's a bad person, and I still haven't figured out how he's tracking me.

But seeing his accomplishments online brings up more questions. Had he ever used dream psychology on me? Is that why he's so interested in my dreams and the nightmares I face about being a child?

"This is a bad idea," I mutter, and reach for my cell phone on the end table. I have his number, thanks to Melinda giving him mine for therapy, and even though I haven't saved it in my phone, it's easy enough to find in my call history.

I don't have to do this. While I'm itching to ask him something, a few somethings, it's still a bad idea. It's not one I have to follow through with, either.

Still, I hit the call button and wait.

It rings once, and I let out a breath when he doesn't answer.

It rings again, and I rationalize that maybe he just isn't there. Hell, I could hang up before the next ring, before I give him a chance to—

The third ring cuts off, and I hear a long, soft sigh against my ear, along with the sound of someone moving around.

"Every time I think I know what you'll do, you surprise me, Quinn. What do you need?"

I look down, not answering, as I consider his question and why I've even called. I could still hang up, after all. It's not like he can force me to answer over the phone.

When I don't say anything, I expect him to hang up. Curiosity stretches my silence out longer, and all I hear is another exhale and what sounds like dishes clinking.

"Are you at home?" I ask finally, wondering why *that* is my first question. I should just get this over with, not try to make conversation.

"Yes. I'm doing dishes. Why? Do you want to come over?" He asks the question lazily, as if it doesn't matter to him either way. Maybe it doesn't.

"Has Clara seen your house yet?" It's rude to answer him with questions, but I don't exactly care about manners right now.

"No. Would it make you jealous if she had?"

"No. I don't care."

"Liar." Amusement touches his tone, and a faucet comes on somewhere near the phone. *"You're not in trouble, are you? I don't mind playing whatever game this is, but I want to make sure you're alright."*

"What are you going to do if I say no and tell you that I've been kidnapped by a drug cartel and shipped to South America?" I ask, my words dry.

"Come find you, kill them all, and bring you home."

"What if I want to stay and rule over them?"

"Then I'll make you their queen." The words aren't what I expect. He said it all so casually, like murder isn't the most unhinged thing in the world to discuss. Especially when he *is* a murderer, so it's not as hypothetical as when other people mention it.

"How would you kill them?" I don't know why I ask. Especially when my words come out soft, almost whispered, instead of in the deadpan tone I intend. Why do I care how he'd kill them?

"*Is this your phone sex talk? If so, I have to admit, it's really doing it for me, Quinn.*" I don't reply. Instead, I listen to him do his dishes, the sound of his off key whistling going in and out of my ears. Finally, I hear the faucet turn off, and after a few seconds of footsteps on his fancy hardwood floors, it sounds like he sits.

"How would you kill them?" I repeat, in case he's somehow forgotten the question.

"*You know how I'd do it.*"

"Do I?"

"*Oh, I see. You're not really asking for the information, are you?*" His voice deepens, the sound husky and velvety. If I were in the room, I'm sure I'd be able to hear his amusement more clearly, or see it in the warmth of his brown eyes. "*You just want to hear me talk about it. If I tell you, will you tell me why you've called? I know it's not for this, though I certainly don't mind answering your questions.*"

"I might," I reply, words clipped as I shrug. He can't see the movement, obviously, but that's not relevant right now. I can barely think straight, let alone figure out why I'm doing this apart from some weird, sick fascination that I need to get checked out by a doctor.

"*I'd cut them to pieces for you. I know you've seen the work my claws can do. I could rip them apart, or just slice them up. I like the freedom to explore my options.*"

"What..." I swallow hard, hating that my heart is in my throat and my thighs are pressed together around the warmth pooling in my lower body. "What do your claws look like?" Until now I hadn't been sure of his murder weapon of choice.

Why hasn't he shown them to me, if he cares so much and wants me to feel the same for him as he does for me?

"*Come over and find out.*"

"Not on my life." I laugh, the sound grating and sharp. "I'm not that stupid."

"*Then tell me why you're calling, Quinn. Unless it really is just so I can get you off with murder talk. Are you wet for me yet?*" My stomach twists at the question, delivered in that same silky tone.

There's no way in hell I'm going to answer.

"Do you know anything about Ashwick?" It isn't the question I want to ask so badly, but it'll do. "It's in Indiana, and—"

"*I know where Ashwick is,*" Gabriel responds calmly. "*And I know it's full of killers.*"

"What do you mean?"

"*I mean what I said. If you're planning a vacation there, I'd like to advise you against it. I've worked too hard to lose you to a town of crazies.*"

What he said doesn't make sense. There's no way an entire town is full of killers, but I push his jokes out of my head. "Mr. Durham, the guy you threw into a wall, came to talk to me today. You could've listened in, if you weren't talking to your girlfriend about your date. How'd it feel when she was undressing you with her eyes?"

He makes a grating sound that might be a chuckle, and sighs. "*You're jealous.*"

"Of what?"

The silence rings between us, turning my stomach a few times. "No, I'm not jealous, Gabriel." The words don't feel authentic, they don't ring true in my ears. I hate them when I say them, and hope he doesn't see it too.

"*He came to talk to you about Ashwick? About how people whisper about copycats around here, because the two places are within a few hours of each other?"* There's patience in his voice that grates on me, and I grit my teeth together at having the big reveal stolen from me.

"Something like that. Did you know they closed the investigation really fast on the Birkins? And that they're basically keeping it out of the news? I went to their house the other day—"

It's impossible not to hear the surprised noise from his side of the phone, nor the way that he murmurs something that might not be a compliment.

"*Anyway.* Their bedroom is cleaned out. Just their bedroom. Don't you think that's weird?"

"*I think you're very obsessed with murder for someone trying to prove to me she doesn't want to be a part of it.*" I don't expect those words. My fingers feel cold, and I nearly drop the phone in surprise. The memories he brings back assault my minds' eye, and I nearly hang up on him.

"Don't say that," I snap finally. "Don't say shit like that, Gabriel."

"*As you wish, Quinn.*" He certainly doesn't sound too put out about it. "*Are you trying to ask me if I want to start a Scooby Gang with you so we can go investigate a murder?*"

"I never said I wanted to do it with *you.*"

Silence on the line makes me wonder if he's hung up. I open my mouth to speak, and I check the phone once to make sure he's still there. "Gabriel?" I ask finally, tentatively. Have I upset him?

"*No,*" he says at last. "*I'm not going to ask. I shouldn't have to. But you shouldn't be so fired up to investigate a murder like that. Especially alone. Do you hear me, Quinn? I'm saying no.*"

"I'm not asking your *permission!*" I snap back, losing my temper. "That's not why I called you. You're not my parent or guardian, Gabriel. I don't need—"

"*You're mine,*" he reminds me smoothly. "*And I'm telling you no, you aren't going off alone. Mine or not, what if you find something? What if you end up dead?*"

"Then I guess you'll have to find someone else to obsess over!"

"*That'll never happen.*" He lets out a long sigh, and I can picture him pinching the bridge of his nose. "*I don't wish to argue with you. Not about this. If you want to discuss it, you can come over. But if this is all you want—*"

"It's not," I interrupt, kicking myself for sounding so eager. "Don't hang up. Please." The word nearly kills me to say, and his silence makes me nervous. "Gabriel?"

"*I'm still here. What else do you want, princess?*" The nickname kicks something in me into high gear, but I refuse to think about it.

"Do you remember the first time we met? In your office?"

"*Of course I do.*"

"You told my case worker that you didn't have time to take on another foster kid. Remember?"

"*I sure do.*"

"But you did anyway. Can I ask you why?" There are a ton of things I want to ask, and this wasn't the one I'd planned, but now that I'm here, I find that I can't help myself.

He takes his time in answering. I hear him shift, and wonder if he's sitting at his desk or his big leather couch. "*Because you needed me,*" he says finally. "*More than anyone else I was seeing, you needed me. You walked into my office with a black eye and a chip on your shoulder that was dragging you to your knees.*"

"That sounds like every foster kid I know," I point out. "And not that special."

"*But you came into my office with violence in your eyes, and promised me you didn't need me. You said you would never let your-*"

self be hurt again, no matter what, and that you could deal with your trauma on your own."

I barely remember that day. I *do* recall what he's talking about, only because I'd waited until my social worker was gone until I'd had the guts to say it to the nice, well-dressed man who'd agreed to be my temporary therapist. I'd been shitty, and he... hadn't.

"I can't believe you remember that," I mutter, picking at a loose string in my tee. "That's so random."

"No, it isn't. Do you know what I was worried about back then? Do you know why I agreed to take you as a client, then kept you?"

"Because you're kind of insane, and you saw some broken kid with a messed up life?" I assume. That's all I was back then, after all. Especially before he helped me.

"Because *I saw a girl who was planning a murder.*"

His words make me go cold. This time the phone does fall from my hand, and it clatters to the floor as I close my eyes hard.

It's not true.

If I leave the phone on the floor long enough, surely he'll hang up. Except, when I pick it up again, he hasn't. Sucking in a breath, I put it to my ear and say, softly, "You're lying. You're trying to freak me out."

"Am I?" There's something there, in his voice, that I don't want to think about. That I don't want to remember. *"Are you sure you don't want to come over? I can help you work through this."*

"There's nothing to work through."

"Only because you don't want to remember."

"*Shut up!*" I snap, nearly throwing the phone this time. "There's nothing to fucking remember, Gabriel. Nothing to work through. I'm sick of you doing this to me. I'm sick of you following me around and pretending I'm something I'm not. Can't you just leave me alone?!" I lunge to my feet, unable to sit still as my heart pounds with the fear I always try to pretend I don't feel.

"*No, I can't,*" he says, just so simply. "*I'll never leave you alone, Quinn. And I'll never let you go. And not because you were the girl who wanted to murder everyone who did her wrong. Do you remember the dreams you used to have?*"

"Shut up," I whisper, eyes closing hard. This had been such a bad idea. Everything about this call was terrible, and my body begs for a way to escape his words and the memories he brings to my mind.

"*Do you remember the ones about the bad house?*"

"No."

"*Because I remember that it used to not be me that killed your foster father in the end.*"

I can't do this. I won't, and I'm glad that he isn't in the room with me. Instead of answering, or letting him keep talking, I hang up on him and chuck my phone to the sofa, hoping it gets lost in the threadbare cushions and falls into some black hole.

I won't do this with him. I won't do it with myself, either.

No matter what he says, or does, I'm not the girl he remembers, or the girl I think he wants me to be.

CHAPTER
SEVENTEEN

H e gasps when I stab him. My foster father's mouth falls open, and blood leaks from his eyes like tears.

"Why?" he coughs, though there's no fear or apology in his face or the word. "Why, why, WHY—" When he tries to step forward I stab him again, this time in the throat, and blood spatters my face and chest. It's hot enough to burn, though the feeling is distant and somewhere in the back of my head, it hits me that I'm dreaming.

Hadn't I been guided through this dream before?

I step back once, then again, as my foster father crawls toward me. His breath rattles too loudly, and the blood in his eyes turns them red as he just keeps coming.

Still I stumble backward, the knife falling to clatter on the landing beside me. He shouldn't be able to catch me, but I feel like I'm slowing down, as though I'm moving through molasses.

Finally, I can't move at all. My heart pounds, fear coursing through my veins as I stare at him, and one hand reaches out and up. He claws his way up my body, dragging me down until my knees hit the floor hard and one of his hands can curl around my throat.

He squeezes, and his smile widens. It hurts more than anything else here. The pain is real, instead of distant, and my blood burns in my veins. My foster father's face morphs, turning younger, until Billy Owens sneers in my face, blood pouring from him.

"Wake up, Quinn," he hisses in my face, spattering me with bloody saliva. "Wake up, wake up, wake up—"

My eyes fly open, and I sit up with a gasp. Or rather, I try to. A warm, heavy weight pushes me back down, and for a brief, terrifying moment I see my foster father above me, his bloody visage leering down at me.

Lightning flashes in the room, coming through a large bay window that isn't mine. That sends my heart into overdrive, and when my eyes lock on a familiar face, the comfort that runs through my veins is embarrassing.

"Gabriel," I whisper, my hands coming up to his face. I need to touch him, to touch something real, even as thunder crashes outside.

"Shh, Quinn," he murmurs, letting me pull his face down to mine. "Shh, it's okay. You're awake now."

"I dreamed of him." My heart still beats rabbit-fast in my chest, only encouraged by the storm as my hands dig into his hair. "I couldn't help it, and I didn't want to. I killed him again, like I did when I was younger. But he wouldn't stay dead, he just kept coming, and—" I'm barely sure who I'm talking about, as my brain remembers the man in my dream as both my foster father *and* Billy. "I killed him," I whisper, hands tightening on the sheets around me. "I did—"

He shushes me gently, and when I squirm on the plush bed, I realize that not only is it not mine either, but his knee is pressed between my thighs. Every bit of my body suddenly focuses on that fact, and remembers how good he'd made me feel in his office not that long ago.

"You're okay," Gabriel murmurs. "You're all right. It was

just a dream, and he can't hurt you. If you stab him, he'll be well and truly dead, princess." He leans close, until I can feel his breath on my lips, and hesitates only to meet my eyes before he kisses me.

Kisses from Gabriel are never sweet, and this one turns filthy moments after it begins. His tongue coaxes mine against it, and when he pulls it back it's only so he can nip and worry at my lips. But in the silence broken only by my gasps and the thudding of my heart, I finally realize what it means that this isn't my bedroom.

"Where am I?" I try to sit up, only for him to push me back down again. "This isn't my house."

His grin is slow to curl over his lips, and not the least bit apologetic. "I knew you'd have trouble tonight," he replies, as if it's an answer. "I thought I'd make sure to be here for you."

"But *here* should've been my house."

"You're such a heavy sleeper," he goads, and he can't help the dark amusement on his features now. "I thought for sure I'd wake you up. I thought for sure you *knew*. But you never did. Even though I carried you out of your house and put you in the back seat. You never woke up. Not *once*."

"You kidnapped me?" I repeat, trying to remember any of what he'd said. "You *kidnapped me?*"

"Yeah, Quinn." He doesn't even try to deny it. "And it was so *fucking easy*. I knew you'd sleep better in my bed, and I was mostly right. It wasn't until the storm that you started having nightmares." As I try to collect my thoughts, he buries his face in my neck. "And you look so fucking cute when you're asleep."

"You kidnapped me." I'm still stuck on that fact, though instead of increasing, the fear in my chest is ebbing away. "Did you drug me?"

"I didn't need to," he replies with a soft laugh. "Isn't that fucked up? I didn't even *need to* drug you."

"You're…" There isn't a word that I can think of to express my opinion of him, but I try anyway. "You're fucked up. Insane. You can't kidnap me!" I shove against him, though there's not enough conviction there to convince myself I don't love the feel of his teeth grazing against my throat.

"Tell me all about it," he purrs. "Come on, Quinn. Convince me that you're upset with me." He sits up, giving me room to maneuver, though doesn't move the leg that's still pressed flush against me. "I'd give you a knife; if I didn't have to go to the kitchen to get it. Do you want to hurt me, Quinn?"

"Yes," I whisper, my chest heaving as I look at him. I shouldn't feel this way about him. I shouldn't be burning up under him, and aware of every tiny movement of his leg against my body. Really, I should be screaming, looking for my phone, and knocking him out with the nearest coffee mug.

I try to sit up, but he shoves me back down with a hand on my throat. "A couple of rules, my vicious darling," he hums, and the look in his eyes is something I've never seen before. It's hard to reconcile this dark, terrifying person above me with *Gabriel,* though I've known this about him all along. "If you leave this room, the game's over. If you can't answer me when I ask if you're alright, it's over. Understand?"

"What if I don't want to play with you?" *I do.* I do, and that's such a fucked up problem that feels like it'll have to wait. At least until the sun rises.

"Then prove it."

My hand comes up and I try to sit up again, this time mostly succeeding as I reach for the neck of his tee. I snag the fabric, just enough, and he's forced to sit back on the bed, no longer pinning me in place.

When he hesitates, I lunge forward, my hand at his throat as I shove him down onto the king size bed. I know he lets me, because he's never this easy, and I end up straddling his waist, my knees pinning his arms as I look down at him.

But he doesn't fight me. His gaze is bright with interest, and under me I can *feel* that he's into this as well. "How dare you?" I whisper, my trembling hand fisting in his shirt. "Why would you *kidnap me*, Gabriel?"

The burning in my body isn't anger now, though. At least, not entirely. My other hand comes up, and I grip his throat the way I had before. The way he does it to me that makes me light-headed enough to feel amazing afterward.

He doesn't even resist. He lets me, his head falling back to give me better access.

"How dare I?" he asks, sounding only mildly inconvenienced. "I can do whatever I want with you. *Whenever* I want. And I wanted you here, in my bed. Not in that shit stain of a house next to a neighbor that's begging for a blade in her chest."

"She never did anything to you," I hiss, trembling. "Why would you—"

"Maybe I'm just jealous that she gets to be near you." When I tighten my grip, he takes it as some kind of sign. Gabriel suddenly flips us, throwing me onto the bed so I'm on my hands and knees, before gripping my hair and forcing my face against the mattress. "Maybe I hate that she has so much access to you, when I'm all the way on the other side of town?"

"Maybe you're inventing reasons." My voice shakes, but I can't tell if it's from fear or excitement. Or both.

He snickers, his voice sounding closer than I'd expected, and suddenly, he bites down hard on my shoulder. "Maybe I am," he teases in my ear. "Maybe I'm just looking for any reason to claim you as mine again. You left so fast last time. I was hurt." Without warning, he grips my shirt, and I feel something sharp against my skin that makes me still.

"Wait—"

"I'm not going to hurt you," he says carefully. "And I'll replace what I cut within the week, I promise. Do you understand?"

I do, but I can't help the shiver that goes through me. Especially when he tightens his grip, and I realize exactly what he's going to do.

"I need something to wear, Gabriel," I whisper, clenching my fingers in the sheets under me. I'm too nervous to really protest, when he has something that feels like a knife. "Please, I need—"

He's not listening, or he doesn't care. There's a loud ripping sound, and moments later my old, ratty sleep shirt is pulled off of me in pieces.

"You don't need anything, princess," Gabriel replies, fingers catching the waistband of my shorts. "If you have it, then you'll just hide from me. And I would rather you didn't."

"Just let me take them off." I could tell him to stop. I could get up and head for the door, and I'm confident he'd let me.

I could tell him not to, if I wasn't so invested in what this will feel like.

"I don't want you to go to the trouble," he purrs, and I feel the blade skim my thigh as he lifts the fabric away from my skin. "But try to convince me, anyway."

"It's easier, and I can't stay here forever." The fabric is tight against my skin where he's pulling it, and I flinch away from the touch of his knuckles. "I need something to wear to work."

"Yeah," he replies, oh so agreeably. "I guess I didn't think of that. What will the neighbors think, right? What if this just means that you can never leave, ever again? You have a point, Quinn. A really excellent one."

"So you'll let me take them off?"

His answer is a snort, and the sound of tearing fabric again.

The blade parts the thin fabric easily, and when my shorts are done being given the same treatment as my shirt, he tugs them off of me as well and sits back and presses me to my belly against the bed.

"So gorgeous." There's a kind of reverence in his voice that I don't expect, and when I try to move, he presses a hand to my lower spine. "No, princess. Just stay there for me, all right? Just let me play with you a little."

The knife comes down next, trailing down my spine and up over my ass until it's skimming the top of my thighs. I can't help the small sounds that leave me as the blade dips between my thighs slightly, but he only huffs a soft laugh and drags it back up my body again, never once doing more than teasing.

"So docile with a blade against your skin," he teases, leaning over me once more. "Is it because you're afraid I'll cut you? Or because of how much you like it." The knife clatters to the table beside the bed and he grips my hips, moving enough to drag me to my knees.

"I don't like it," I lie, trying to sit up, only for my face to be shoved back down.

"Normally I like to look at you, but I think this once you're better right there. Right here, under me, where you belong." I can barely move, especially when he fists a hand in my hair to keep me with my ass in the air and my face against his super soft pillowcase.

"Bite me," I mutter sarcastically, closing my eyes hard. A second later I shriek, having not expected him to actually sink his teeth into my hip.

"Tell me to do it again," he invites. "Tell me all the wicked things you'd like for me to do." When I shake my head he bites me again, this time worrying at the spot and sucking a bruise onto my skin that I have a feeling will be there for days.

"I bet you're wet for me," he goads, fingers finding my slit. "I bet you're soaked, aren't you?"

"It's from the violence, not for you," I snap in reply, relaxing my shoulders when his hand leaves my hair.

"Oh, yeah?" He leans over me again, and I tense when I expect another bite. Except, it never comes. He settles behind me again, and his fingers dig into my hip when I try to look over my shoulder.

"Stay where you are, Quinn. Stay where you are and let me play with you, or I'll have to handcuff you. Do you think I won't? Do you think I wouldn't enjoy you helpless and writhing on my bed? With no clothes and no one to come looking for you?" He snorts at his own words. "I'm still willing to let you go when I'm done, but if I have you handcuffed on my bed like a sweet, willing little pet... I don't know if that'll still be the case."

"You can't keep me here forever."

"I most certainly can."

The blade of the knife touches my inner thigh, and I cry out against the pillow. He doesn't give me a chance to move, however. He's positioned so that he can grip my hair and push down against my back, while still running the blade along my inner thighs.

"What are you doing?" I demand, wishing I could at least turn and look at him. "Gabriel—"

"I'm giving you what you want," he replies, all innocence. "I'm giving you what you *told me* you wanted. You like the violence. You like the knife, right?" The blade disappears, and I nearly scream when something other than his fingers finds my slit.

With a jolt, I realize it's the handle of the knife. I bury my face in the pillow, my thighs trembling as he pushes it into me.

He's right about how wet I am, because the hilt slides into my pussy smoothly.

"Good girl," Gabriel purrs, still holding me with a hand on my upper back, just between my shoulder blades. "Good *fucking* girl, taking this for me." His movements speed up, impatience lacing them, and I close my eyes hard at the idea of coming on the handle of a knife.

"Do you want me to make you come like this?" he taunts, as if he can read my thoughts. "You want to come on a knife? That's fucked up, Quinn."

"That's not what I want," I hiss, fingers clenched hard against the pillow. Heat pools in my stomach as he fucks me with it, and I can feel just how wet I am. It doesn't help that I can hear it, too, and the sound of the knife going in and out is loud in my ears. "Please, Gabriel—"

"You don't want it? You don't want to come all over my knife, my gorgeous girl?" I hate the way he taunts me. And the way it makes something curl in my stomach that's impossible to ignore. "Well, you know what the alternative is, don't you?"

"Anything," I gasp out, feeling the way I clench around the knife involuntarily.

"Anything? Anything at all?" He doesn't wait for me to reply. The knife is thrown across the room, clattering to the floor as Gabriel moves. He's behind me seconds later, and through the rain that's pounding against the window to my left, I hear the sound of his clothes being shoved out of the way.

By the time he's draped over me once more, his shirt is gone. His skin is so warm against mine, and he feels like a burning line of heat against my body. His cock brushes my slit, and he teases me, guiding it against me but only letting it dip into me before he's back to teasing.

I whine, hating how much I need him. "Fuck me," I tell him, mind spinning. "Hurry up and *fuck me.*"

"I should make you say please," he sneers against my ear, but when I open my mouth to reply he suddenly slams into me, causing me to choke on a gasp. "But I like you desperate and demanding. You're so needy. Has no one ever fucked you properly before?" His movements are never slow or gentle. He starts off rough and keeps going, dragging gasps and cries from my lips as he fucks me.

"Not like you," I say, lifting my head so he can more easily wrap his fingers around my throat. I expect him to tease, to just remind me he's there.

I don't expect the force of his grip that nearly makes me see stars.

"Gabriel—"

"Trust me," he growls against my ear, his other hand circling my hip to find my clit. He circles it with one finger, and he's just as rough with his teasing as he is with the rest of me. Yet, I can't find the breath to complain. I can't find the desire to, either, as he treats me like a toy he can use to his contentment.

When my vision starts to blur, I choke out a protest that goes ignored. The anger that's kept me warm this whole time dulls, until the only thing that's keeping me warm is his body against mine, and the way he fucks me.

"It feels so good this way," he promises. "Don't worry, Quinn. I won't hurt you. I just want to feel you gasping, feel your pulse. It's so fast, like you're going to run away from me. But you're not, are you?" I can't respond now. Not when the only thing holding me up is Gabriel.

"You'll never run away from me again." His fingers tighten under my jaw and I feel myself slipping out of consciousness, just as his movements tip me over the edge.

Instantly he lets go and I gasp, my orgasm *ripping* through me so hard that tears stream from my eyes, staining his pillowcase. I can only grip his sheets and try not to shatter into a million pieces as I come, and focus on his long, uneven thrusts until finally he buries himself in my body and comes as well.

Gabriel's teeth close against the skin of my throat, a soft sound trickling from between them as he coaxes a mark into my skin, so close to the spot he loves to choke me.

"Next time, I'll let you rip me to shreds," he promises, as my brain gives up the fight with consciousness. I'm exhausted, oxygen deprived, and I can feel myself slipping back into sleep as he rolls onto his side and pulls me against him without pulling out.

"Next time, I'll let you do whatever you want to me."

I groan, turning my face into the pillow and try to move, only for him to hold me tight against him. It isn't uncomfortable. In fact, it's anything but.

"No, you don't have to move," he laughs softly against my skin. "I like you right here, full of my cum, and where I know you aren't going anywhere, Quinn."

"Have to work tomorrow," I mumble, eyes still closed. "I gotta go home."

"No, you really don't."

I want to argue. I want to tell him that I most certainly do… but I can't. Not when he's so warm and the blanket he pulls up to my shoulders feels so heavy that I don't want to move. I let him pull me against him, until he's lying half over me and still inside of me, but by the time he leans forward to whisper in my ear again, I'm so far gone that I can't hear what it is he's said.

I'll just have to remember to ask him in the morning.

EIGHTEEN

When my phone rings, it occurs to me that I wasn't in a position to have brought it here last night. Still, it drags me from my sleep and I crack my eyes open to see that it's sitting on the end table, plugged in.

Not only that, but Gabriel is no longer in the bed with me. I hate that I feel disappointed. That something in me uncurls, and my morning is suddenly sort of ruined.

I shouldn't feel like this about a man who has kidnapped me, chased me across the country, and hasn't given me any real reason to return his feelings.

His feelings.

That twists me up inside too, even as I grope for the phone on the nightstand. He's never been clear about his feelings, except to tell me he thinks I'm his, that I belong to him. Is that it? Is he just some crazy guy I should've turned into the cops a long time ago?

Yeah, probably.

"Hello?" I murmur, still unsure where Gabriel has gone to.

Downstairs, probably. And I suppose I should be grateful that I didn't wake up on the curb.

Not that he's ever given me a hint that he would do that to me.

A door behind me opens, just as Melinda's voice finds my ears. *"I'm sorry to call you so early, Quinn."* She sounds as apologetic as humanly possible, and a hint of worry comes across, even through our bad connection. *"But I need to ask you for a favor. Is that okay? You're not out of town, are you?"*

Thunder rumbles in the distance, like a far off reminder of last night's storm, or the promise of another one today. The bed dips behind me, and with a sigh, Gabriel drapes himself over me, kissing my arm.

So he hadn't abandoned me after all.

"I'm here. I'm not at home right now, though." I narrow my eyes, looking over my shoulder toward Gabriel as he nips and kisses his way down my arm. As I look at him, my eyes catch sight of the knife on the dresser across the room.

Is it the knife from last night?

"I hope everything is alright. And I'm so sorry if I'm ruining your morning." She sighs and hesitates before going on. *"Do you remember Lily?"*

I tense under Gabriel's touch, and I can tell immediately that he feels it. His touches pause, his mouth leaving my skin, and he snags an arm around my waist to pull me back against him.

Instantly, it's pretty clear that he's not wearing any clothes. I take a sharp breath, eyes closing, and try to focus on what's being said to me, instead of his body against my own. "I remember." How could I not? I'd felt so bad for the girl, and I'd seen myself in her more than I care to admit.

"She needs to be picked up. I'm not sure what happened. A relative came by for a visit that wasn't approved by us... I don't know

exactly. She's safe, from what I understand. But she's at the Easter County office and needs to be picked up in an hour." I have no idea where that is, though it can't be more than a thirty-minute drive, but that's why god made the Maps app and gave it GPS capabilities.

"It'll take me a little bit to get there. I have to go home and, umm..." I trail off when Gabriel nudges my arm, pointing toward the window. Just under it, on the padded seat, is a stack of clothes that look suspiciously like they came from my house.

What a creep. A thoughtful creep, but a creep anyway.

"Never mind, I don't have to. I can leave soon." I say, because I feel the way Gabriel doesn't care about a dire situation. No, he's just really happy to be in bed with me. His hips move against mine, rocking slowly, and it's not exactly a hardship for me to allow him to hook a hand under my knee and pull it up over his thigh. "Can I ask... she's your case, right?" I don't want to accuse her of putting off her work, but this isn't the first time I've had to do something for her, or the second.

The Birkins come to mind, along with Lily's first pick up. Those are, or were in one case, Melinda's cases.

So why are they getting dumped on me?

Gabriel's getting more insistent; his kisses on my neck pick back up as his teeth graze the mark he'd left last night. I shudder under the feel of it, my skin still oversensitive from his bites.

"She is." Melinda doesn't sound angry. She just sounds... tired. *"But I'm maxed out on overtime for the month. I'm sorry to drop this on you, Quinn. I know I need to hire another social worker for the office. If you know anyone, point them my way, I guess."* She laughs, but the sound is absent of actual humor. Again, she radiates tiredness and being overworked.

My heart sinks for her, and I reach up to grip Gabriel's hair, hoping he'll get the memo and *stop* for a second.

He does, surprising me. His movements slow until all I can feel is his breathing against my back. "I'll be there soon, okay?" I ask, hating how I'm so easy to convince. Especially since I know this will be just as difficult as the first time. That Lily's case is going to hurt me all over again. I know that, just as much as I know I'll jump at any opportunity to help her, because she reminds me of me in all the wrong ways.

"*Thank you, Quinn.*" She sounds relieved, and I hear the squeak of her office chair as she sits back into it. "*I'm making some calls to see if I can get someone else to go out with you. Like I said, everything should be fine. But lately...*" she trails off, and Gabriel's patience wanes. He bites down on my throat, pulling a gasp from me that I cover with a cough. "*Things are weird lately,*" she says at last, acting as if she hadn't noticed the sound. "*Call me when you're there. I'm working out where to take her, but I'll know by then.*"

"N-no problem." I hate the unsteadiness in my voice, and when Gabriel's length brushes my slit, I fight hard not to make a sound to betray my feelings. "I'll be there soon." Hanging up more quickly than is polite, I'm suddenly pulled onto my back, the movement surprising me into releasing a gasp.

"You're impatient," I mutter spitefully as Gabriel reaches out to press a hand against my sternum. He jerks me to him with the other hand until one of my legs is up over his shoulder and my other knee is pressed to his hip.

"You let her ask too much of you," he replies, his length sinking into me without hesitation. I choke on the air I'd been breathing, but I can't do more than grab his wrist, nails sinking into his skin, as he holds me in place to fuck me. "It's your day off. You should've told her no."

My hips rock into his, then my eyes find his gaze and

narrow. "Maybe I'm just trying to get away from you sooner," I say, though it's pretty clear by the situation that I'm not.

He lifts a brow, hand pressing harder so I can't arch up at all. "Somehow, I don't think that's true. But would you like me to hurry up? I could just use you for myself, come inside this sweet cunt, and leave you aching for the whole day. Is that what you *want*, Quinn?" He punctuates each word with a hard thrust that shakes my entire being. "For me to leave you needy and dripping with cum all day?"

Yes, please is obviously the wrong answer, and I shouldn't say it.

"Do it," I dare, still gripping his arm tightly as he hitches my leg higher over his shoulder so he can drive more deeply into me. "*Do it*, if you want. I'll just finish myself off later. I did just buy fresh batteries, after all. And I'm really good at knowing what I want."

His smile is rueful, eyes glittering. "You're such a little monster," the bane of my existence purrs. "You know that?"

"Only when it involves *you*."

My leg drops from his shoulder as he lunges forward, hand moving to pin my wrists above my head harshly. He kisses me, biting down on my lip with a growl before using his free hand to grab my throat and hold me exactly where he wants me.

I return the sound with a snarl of my own, nipping at his tongue when it enters my mouth. I'm met with a careful squeeze of his fingers, and his thrusts becoming harder, more erratic. If he's close, then so am I, but I don't want to be the one to come first. Not with him, not this time.

"Are you close?" I taunt, when he pulls back for air. I lunge upward as much as I can, teeth coming together with a sharp *click* as I miss his lip with my bite. He laughs darkly, and kisses me again, forcing my mouth open wide to feed me the noises he makes.

"You're just as close," he tells me, his words teasing while his tone is more or less a growl. "I wondered for a long time what it would be like to fuck you. What you'd get off on. Turns out, you really do just like it when I'm rough. I don't need to play with your clit or whisper sweet words to you, do I?"

"You could try. Who knows? I might *like it*," I lie, knowing that he's right.

It's this that I love. More than anyone else I've ever slept with, Gabriel knows how to get me off. His personality, his actions. The way he's so dominating and rough yet playful, really does it for me.

Does that make me just as fucked up as him?

My release catches me by surprise just as Gabriel's teeth close over my nipple. His hand leaves my throat, coming down to play with the other just as harshly, and even though I can tell he tries, he can't hold back as my knees tighten around his body, pulling him close as I come.

He curses softly, turning to pant against my neck as he presses close against me. My hands flex in his grip, but he doesn't let go. Not until he's well and truly spent and can sit up to look down at me, eyes glittering.

"What?" I snap, suddenly self-conscious as the last of my orgasm tingles down my spine. "Why are you looking at me like that? And I swear to God, if it's some cheesy fucking line that involves the word 'mine,' then—"

"I was just looking at you, Quinn," Gabriel chuckles, cutting me off with his light words. "Don't read so much into it. I just really like looking at you."

"Yeah?" I ask, falling back down onto my back. "Why?"

"Because you're beautiful."

Anything I want to say is choked off in my throat. All the comebacks I have go out the window as he looks at me. I can't tear my eyes off of him. From his golden skin, or the tattoos that litter his arms. *He's gorgeous.*

So why am I just now noticing it?

"I..." I lick my lips, knowing that I need to say *something*. I can't just lay here, looking and feeling dumbfounded.

Say something.

Say anything at all.

My mouth opens, even though I don't know what to say, but thankfully I'm interrupted by the ring of his phone.

Gabriel sighs and leans over me to the nightstand, picking it up before sitting between my thighs once more. "Hello?" he asks, back to his professional voice even as his hand wanders up my leg. "Oh. Hey, Melinda." His eyes find mine, and I'm sure my gaze reflects his confusion. "Sure, I have a minute. What do you need?"

CHAPTER
NINETEEN

I don't know what to tell Melinda, other than the same phrase I've been repeating in different ways for the last few minutes.

"It... went okay," I say, tapping my fingers against the armrest of the stiff chair. "I didn't really need G—Dr. Brooks, though," I say, hoping I haven't slipped up by nearly saying his first name.

After being called by Melinda to go pick up Lily in the rain, he'd been the one to convince me that his car was better than mine, and she'd like it more.

Though it had taken me until we'd gotten there and I'd seen Lily's new foster mom watching her stand in the storm while the woman glared from the porch, to realize why bringing Gabriel was a good idea.

He'd been livid. All righteous, therapist fury and citing laws the woman was breaking. She'd started off defiant, trying to poke holes in his argument. But Gabriel had never been easily breakable. Especially when he was upset.

"How is he doing now, anyway? You're seeing him for therapy, yes? He said that's where you were this morning when I called, and that's why you were both so quick to get there together." She smiles kindly, with an invitation for me to tell her the truth. Like she won't fire me for fucking the older therapist.

Will she?

I blink up at her, trying to figure out what to say. Trying to figure out how much she knows about us. Does she know Gabriel had to hold me away from the woman, because I'd been threatening to take away every child in her care and each cent of state funding she received for them?

Or does she know I sat in the back with Lily, letting her cry into my hoodie while I wondered why Melinda couldn't bother to show up and do something about the situation? It was *her* *case*. Hers, not ours. She should've been the one to rush out there, to protect Lily before anything had happened.

It shouldn't have been pawned off on the two of us, no matter how much it had my blood rushing through my body and causing my hands to curl into fists at the thought. I suck in a deep breath, trying to drag my thoughts away from my irritation, and focus on her words again.

"You know, I'm inviting him to our next pool party. It's in a couple of weeks at the house. We normally have them once a month, but we were working on the liner this time around. Pools." She huffs, throwing one hand up in the air like it's obvious to the world that pools are the bane of her existence. I don't say that she could use her evening hours, since she's always up like a creature of the night, but instead I just smile blithely.

"I wouldn't know," I laugh, knowing I sound uncomfortable. "I've never lived somewhere with a pool." Frankly, I wouldn't know the first thing about them.

"I'm always covered in the smell of chlorine at night," she

adds, shaking her head. "It's dreadful. My husband and I both. Honestly, I'm surprised you haven't noticed it here."

"I don't notice anything," I assure her, wondering why this matters. "I've only smelled chlorine at public pools and..." Blinking, a frown touches my lips as a memory interrupts my thought process.

A pool isn't the only place I've smelled chlorine.

Still, I can't figure out exactly where I've smelled the pool-like scent before. It's been a long time since I've been to a dirty, kid-filled, county run public pool. At least ten years, if not a few more. But the scent of chlorine is sharp in my nose, like it's been a few weeks, instead of a years.

Why can't I figure this out?

When I realize Melinda is speaking again, I give her another smile and try to look interested. "Like I was saying, thank you for taking care of that issue for me. Lily shouldn't have to be moved again, I don't think. Now she's in a better foster home than I could hope for. She would've been there sooner, but they didn't have any space." She hesitates, her pale eyes finding my face and holding my gaze.

Does she want something from me?

Is there some detail she wants that I haven't told her?

I take in a breath as she watches me, unsure of what it is she's going to say. She doesn't worry, or particularly scare me. How could she, when she barely looks like she could hurt a fly?

"You were in foster care, weren't you?" she asks finally, and I blink in surprise, eyes narrowing. It wasn't in my job application, and I'm not open about the fact. Unless Gabriel has said something, I have no idea how she'd know.

"What?" I murmur finally, unwilling to confirm or deny her accusation. "Why do you say that?"

"Because I know what it looks like," she says, leaning back

in her chair with a sigh. "I know the look, and the reactions of an ex-foster kid. Especially one that never got adopted. You saw the worst parts of our system as a child, didn't you, Quinn?"

Tapping my fingers on the chair, I hold her gaze. I don't know what to say, or how to move forward. Hell, I have no idea what she could gain by bringing this up right now.

"Umm..." I look away from her, biting my lower lip as I cycle through the thoughts that won't stop flitting through my head. It isn't a big secret. She's not wrong, obviously. And she can't hold it against me. The thing is simply that I don't want to talk about it. "Yeah," I say finally, my voice soft, the word not forthcoming. I don't want to have a heart-to-heart about this, or drag it out. "Is that okay? Is there something that you're worried about, job related for me?"

"No, no, not at all. You're good at your job, Quinn. You're the best hire I've had in a while. The first that's seemed like they'll stick around, too." She gives a sort of chuckle and glances at her computer. "I worry about you," she says at last. "I worry because I think these cases could get to you more than they get to anyone else. Like Clara." She throws a fond smile toward her window, where Clara is probably sitting. "I don't want you to get burned out, okay? But more than that, I don't want *you* to get hurt by these cases."

This is so strange. Have I ever had someone express such care about me so openly? Probably not, except for the social worker that had worked with me as a kid. She'd loved to tell me how things would get better, how I just needed to think positive thoughts and manifest my dreams to come true.

And yet, the only positive thing that had ever manifested for me were the murders of three people. And that wasn't exactly *positive*.

Sucking in a breath, I try not to zone out as Melinda looks

me over with concern, waiting for some kind of answer that I don't know how to give.

"I'm fine," I say at last, each word slow and articulated well. "Really, I *am* okay. I've wanted to do this for my entire life. I've always known I want to help other foster kids. This won't burn me out, or hurt me, or anything else. I'm really okay." The words sound hollow to my ears, and I hate the feeling that brings.

Am I really telling the truth?

Am I sure?

"If you need to leave, if you ever think this isn't for you, I would never hold it against you." She reaches forward, her hand hovering like a limp, levitating fish on my side of her desk. I see what she wants, and I stare at her hand like it's a cobra that might bite.

I don't need to hold her hand. I don't need the comfort she wants to bring.

Still, I fix a smile on my face and do what she wants, letting her cover my hand with her clammy one. I don't like it. I've never been a huge fan of personal touch, and this isn't winning any points on the subject.

"I'm fine," I repeat, trying to sound like I mean it. "And I'll tell you if that changes, all right?"

"All right." She pats my hand and releases me. "I just worry about you, is all. Now, take off the rest of the day. Go get some lunch. Maybe *with* someone?" She winks at me like there's a secret we're both in on, though I'm not sure what it could be. So I smile at her again and get to my feet, nodding my head like her ideas are good.

Then again...

"Have a good day, Melinda," I tell her, waving on my way out of the office and delving my hand into my pocket to grab my phone.

"*Yes, Quinn?*" he answers on the second ring, sounding just as at ease and relaxed as always.

"Are you free, Gabriel?" I ask, almost jogging to my car. "Can I come talk to you, if you are?"

"*I'm free,*" he agrees, curiosity tinging his voice. "*But you can't come over.*"

My steps slow, and my mouth pulls down into a frown. "What?"

"*You can't come over, because I'm taking you out for dinner. I'll text you the address. Sound good?*"

"Depends on where we're going."

He chuckles, and I hate how much I revel in the sound. "*Guess you'll find out.*"

THIS IS WEIRD.

There's no way around the fact that it's weird to be here, in a restaurant that's dedicated to being an 1800s reenactment.

Especially when the person sitting across from me is Gabriel.

It's nice. I won't lie to myself about that. It's definitely one of the prettiest restaurants I've ever been in, the rooms are decorated in different themes and levels of complexity. The servers walking around all look like they've walked out of *ye olde times* in their floral patterned dresses and overalls. With the restaurant smelling of incredible food, homemade bread, and flowers, I can say with ease that I'll never come to a place like this again.

"This feels like a real date," I admit, surprised at myself. Gabriel, across from me, reads his menu slowly, going over the salads before flipping to the page that shows their steak options. Many restaurants I've seen over the past few years look like they're embracing a modern, minimalist feel. Not this place. Photos of the food decorate the laminated pages, and the green edges of the menu are worn from many years of fingers thumbing through them.

"It *is* a real date," Gabriel replies lazily, stretching out his legs under the table until his feet touch mine. I let him, though I glare up at him as his ankle presses against mine.

"Aren't you worried about what people will think?"

He flips a page of his menu and doesn't look up. His eyes are dark with concentration as he reads, and his eternally tousled hair is on point today.

He's gorgeous.

There's no way around the fact that Gabriel Brooks is the most attractive man I've ever met by a long shot.

His foot hooks with mine, jerking me an inch forward in my chair.

"No," he says, looking up at me intently. "Are you? Is this your way of saying I'm too old for you, Quinn?"

Slowly, I shake my head. "Maybe I was just implying that I look like the carefree, casual dating type and all the boys around here are lining up for my number."

"You should get theirs instead," he says, eyes dropping back to the menu.

"And why's that?"

"So I can track them down easier to kill them."

The words cause my stomach to flip, cause me to press my lips together as my insides go from fluttering to crushing nerves. "I don't know how to feel when you talk to me like that," I say finally, being honest with him for the first time. "I don't understand how you're so comfortable with such casual violence. Especially because I know you mean it. You really would kill someone for asking for my number, wouldn't you?"

He doesn't answer as the waitress appears with our drinks in her pink floral dress that nearly drags the ground. She sets down sweet tea in front of me, and water in front of Gabriel. I watch her, noting her smile is wider for him than for me, and she's more enthusiastic about taking his order than she is mine.

But who can blame her?

By the time she's gone, my elbows are resting on the table, and my gaze returns to Gabriel. Without a menu in front of him, his attention is all for me, and a smile plays on his lips.

"Should I kill her?" I ask under my breath, glad we're alone in our room that's dubbed *the garden room*. "For being interested in you? Or Clara?"

"You know, you could," he replies, leaning forward on the table and propping his chin on his hands. "I'd like to watch and record it. I'd probably get off to it once or twice a month. Maybe we could make a hobby of it. I kill someone for you, then you for me. We'll just have to be careful about not leaving a trail."

"Aren't you afraid of getting caught again? Of not getting away so easily this time?" He still hasn't given me a satisfactory answer as to how he got away in Springwood, and I wonder if he'll continue avoiding the subject if I continue asking.

"No. The only complication would be teaching you how to stay out of jail. It's a bit of a puzzle. A game, really, to make sure you're never caught. I'd prefer to stop covering up for you, though I'm sure I'll have to keep you on a leash for a little while. You'd be my little protégé," he muses, his words causing my hands to clench, nails digging into my palms.

"I'm not a killer," I remind him slowly, trying to enunciate every word. "Not by a long shot."

He only eyes me up and down, then takes a long drink of his water. "Let's talk about something else," he suggests, setting it down again. "As much as I love the games and threats you so enjoy, I want to talk about *us*. About you, Quinn."

"I'd rather talk about you. You should tell me all about your awards for dream psychology," I counter, sitting back in my chair.

"Only if you tell me why you want this career to work out so badly. Is it really just that you're trying to save the countless kids in the system like you? The ones who needed help?" He doesn't look away, even when I do. "Or is it that you want vengeance on a broken system?"

"No, that's not—" I swallow hard, still not looking at him. "That's not why. I want to help people, all right?"

"It's going to break you," he tells me quietly. "And I know you see it too." He tries to reach out for me, but I shove his hand away, glaring at him balefully.

"Tell me where the tracker is in my car," I demand, getting the same rueful look in reply.

"No. You'll take it out." He seems affronted by the idea, but a grin crosses his features. "Absolutely not."

"Tell me about dream psychology and why you like it so much."

That gives him pause. He looks down at his hands, tapping his hands on the smooth top of the fake wood table. "I like things that aren't as rational as our waking time," he says finally. "I like to take the puzzle our dreams present and work out the *why*. And I enjoy hearing about people's fucked up dreams." He rewards me with a smile that makes my breath catch in my throat.

"And here I thought you just had a fetish for sleeping people," I say finally, unsure of what to ask.

"Well, that too. I definitely have some sleep related kinks. Any dreams you want to talk about?"

"Yeah, but I'm kind of stuck on your 'sleep kinks,'" I admit, glancing up to make sure no one else is around. As I do, his foot strokes my ankle, pushing the fabric of my legging up slightly so his boot touches skin.

It shouldn't affect me as much as it does, but that seems to be the story of my life when Gabriel is involved.

"They'll scare you," he assures me, though the look on his face doesn't match his words. He *wants* me to ask. More than that, he really wants to tell me.

"Maybe. But I did let you, *you know*, with a knife," I point out sweetly.

He thinks about it, mulling it over in his head before nodding once as if agreeing with himself. "Do you know what somnophilia is?" he asks, leaning close once more.

I wrack my brain for the word, and shake my head.

"It means I'd love to fuck you while you sleep. I want to wreck you while you're still out of it. Breed that pussy all night long and make sure you enjoy every second of it, even though you aren't awake for some of it. Then you'd wake up in the morning oh so thoroughly *fucked* and beg me for more."

"You..." I trail off and run my tongue along my bottom lip, thinking. By his soft, husky tone and the detail of his explanation, it's clear he's thought a lot about this. And if I'm honest with myself, it doesn't exactly scare me. "Have you done it before?" I ask finally. "You seem to have a pretty clear plan for what you want."

He shakes his head before I'm done. "This may come as a shock, but most women want to be fucked while they're awake. Not while they're out of it."

"Well, how 'out of it' are we talking? I like to enjoy sex, and I like to think I'd need to be somewhat awake for that to happen. But I see the appeal of what you're talking about."

His brows climb in surprise, making a break for his bangs. I stop talking, wondering suddenly if this is the first time I've truly surprised him. "Sell me on it," I urge, hooking my foot around *his* ankle for a change. "What makes you think I won't wake up the moment you touch me?"

"I'd give you a sedative," he replies without needing to think about it. "Not something that would have you out cold. Something to give me a little bit of time to play with you, that's all."

"And you wouldn't stop when I wake up?"

He shakes his head, still looking like he doesn't quite believe me.

"I'd let you," I reply at last. "Call me fucked up, but it sounds exciting. It sounds different. I don't know." Then I shrug when his eyes narrow like he thinks I'm going to suddenly tell him I'm lying and cackle at getting his hopes up. "I like to try new things."

"You'd *actually* do it? Knowing what I want to do? Knowing you'll wake up with cum dripping out of you?" he specifies, as if some part of his earlier discussion was unclear.

I tap my knuckles on the table and nod.

"I don't believe you."

"And I don't believe you like me as much as you say." I shrug. "So, there's that."

"You don't?" It's his turn to look confused, more so than he had. "Why?"

"What do you mean, *why*? This is kind of crazy. You explode into my dorm and announce I'm yours after years of maybe stalking me. Please, don't comment on that. Then you follow me here, because there's a tracker in my car, and tell me how I'm *yours*. But what does that mean, exactly?" It's apparently my turn for speeches, and I hate how uncomfortable I am with them. How every word makes me more and more unsure of my convictions. "Until you get bored? Until you get what you want?"

"Until both of us are dead and reunite in whatever's waiting for us afterward," he clarifies, slipping the words in when breathing becomes a necessity. "Did you really think this was temporary, Quinn?"

"Uh, yeah. Kind of thought you were going to kill me, not fuck me." The waitress walks in, thankfully smiling blithely between us, so cluelessly, that I know she hasn't heard a thing. Naturally, she refills Gabriel's drink first, then mine as an afterthought. But I don't mind. Not right now, when there are much more important things to deal with. Things that have my heart pounding like... like I'm afraid.

Like I can't handle hearing the words that Gabriel really *has* just been treating me like a Christmas puppy who will get dropped off at the shelter in four months.

"Quinn..." He leans forward and catches my hands before I can pull away, dragging them across the table as he hooks his foot around my ankle once more. I'm trapped, unless I want to throw myself off my chair. "This isn't temporary. I wouldn't have been following you all this time if it was. When I say you're mine, I mean that in the permanent sense. I mean, *you're mine*, and there's no changing that. Even if you didn't like me. Even if you begged me to leave. I don't think I could. There's no other option for me. You're it."

"That sounds like a love declaration," I choke weakly. "Like you're trying to say something else with those words."

"Love is too healthy of a word for what we have, darling. Love is for people who aren't like us." I don't need to know what he means. I get the picture.

Tentatively, I turn my hands, curling them around his wrists. "What if I'm awful, and you don't know it? You barely know me. Maybe I snore, or I chew with my mouth open."

"Maybe I leave my socks everywhere," he counters.

"That's a killing offense."

He snorts and drags me closer to him, until we're barely a foot apart, lips parting to speak.

Only this time, I beat him to it. "You're going to do the whole 'mine' thing again, aren't you?" I ask dryly, and this close I see the spark of amusement in his gaze.

"Maybe," he admits. "I'm so *sorry* that repeating myself is boring. I'll have to find some new material."

"Maybe Clara will help you out," I suggest wickedly as he lets go, though his foot stays pressed to mine.

"*Clara* is a means to an end, Quinn," he admonishes. "I needed an ally in your office, and it sure as hell wasn't you in the beginning." He breaks off as, again, our waitress comes back. This time, it's with our two steaming plates of food that she sets in front of us. For him, it's the too-thick pork chop. For me, it's chicken smothered in cheese sauce and a loaded baked potato.

"If you need anything else, let me know," the waitress offers, checking our glasses one more time before leaving again.

I pick up my fork, staring at my food, before setting it down again to look up at the man across from me. "Gabriel?" I ask, and he raises a brow as he assesses his food. "Where did we smell chlorine last? I keep thinking that it was recent. But maybe I'm just going crazy."

He thinks about the answer, and when his words aren't immediate, I know it's not going to be him telling me *nowhere*. He appears to struggle with the words, unsure of what to say, before saying, "At the Birkins' house. Their kitchen smelled a bit like chlorine or bleach. It has the same smell."

"That's right," I murmur, stabbing my potato. "Whatever. It's probably nothing. Thanks, though."

He stares at me, as if sure it's not *nothing*. "Did you mean it?" he asks at last, prompting me to glance up.

"Mean what?"

"That you'd be into my somno plan?"

"Oh, yeah. Why wouldn't I be?" The words are brave, gallant even. I *am* into it, but it also makes me nervously excited. It's terrifying in a way. In a lot of ways. But then again, the idea of it hasn't left my mind since he'd brought it up, so maybe he's not the only messed up one here.

BEFORE I CAN GET into my car, Gabriel pushes me up against it, his large body pinning mine there. My brows raise as I look around pointedly, even as he just looks at me.

"There are people here," I point out, fighting the urge to grip his tee and choke him with it. I like the idea too much for it to be from anger. But this really isn't the place to do it.

"I know. And I'm not doing anything. I just want to know if you mean it, or you're just humoring me."

So we're back to this.

"I... I mean it," I say, thinking about my words. "As long as you promise you won't hurt me. Like, *really* hurt me. I like what we do. But I want to be able to choose how far you go with me."

"I wouldn't go further than what we've done."

"Well, again, you've fucked me with a knife hilt, so that's a pretty shitty argument," I point out dryly, one hand wandering up to tangle in his shirt. I watch him as he reaches into his back pocket until he's holding up a small, orange pill bottle. My heart nearly combusts, and I stare at it, suddenly terrified.

"You don't have to," he says, shaking it to show me the two pills in it. "And no, I don't have them for some nefarious purpose. Sometimes *I* need them."

"Guilty conscience?"

"Lifelong insomnia. They'll make you drowsy. You'll be

harder to wake up, but that's it. If you don't take them, then you don't take them. I won't think less of you or leave just because you're not into—"

It feels like a challenge, and I love a challenge. I swipe the bottle out of his hands and shake it, my eyes never leaving his as I yank him down to me, mouth brushing his. "If I do this, then I get to use a knife on *you*," I bargain, kissing the chuckle from his lips.

"I'd let you do that anyway, my vicious little darling." He kisses me again, harder, and it's him that pulls away first, clearing his throat as he regains his composure. "I'll call you later," he offers, and it's clear he wants to kiss me again as I pocket the bottle of pills.

But that's okay, because he's not the only one.

"I might answer," I shrug, loving the look of irritated amusement on his face. "If I'm not busy." In the back of my mind, the thought of chlorine and bleach spins, not leaving me alone. But that's a *me* thing, and not for him. "Thanks for dinner. It was..." I look over the restaurant, brows rising. "The most interesting place I've ever eaten."

"I feel like the bar was low," he points out, but he's already walking away, his hand sliding down my arm. "Have a good night, Quinn."

I salute in response, trying to be as contrary as possible, as he shakes his head and opens his car door to go home.

TWENTY

ow long do they take to kick in? Sitting on my bed, I stare down at the message I've typed out, consider it, and press send. The pills sit ominously in their small bottle on my knee, and I can't begin to control how rapidly my heart pounds in my chest.

I'm terrified, excited, and I feel like I can't breathe. If I do this, it will be hard to go back. I'm committing to the long haul, to the whole thing. At least until I wake up.

He doesn't text back.

Instead, my phone rings, surprising me, and I answer it a second before putting it on speaker. "I wasn't expecting you to call," I admit awkwardly.

"You haven't taken them, have you?" There's a breathless kind of excitement in his voice, and I look out the window at the lightning that occasionally brightens my room.

"No," I say slowly, my heart skipping a beat and launching to my throat. "Do you not want me to anymore?"

"I just want to talk to you first. I want to make sure you're in a

good headspace for this." His words are soothing, kind, and so patient I could chew off my own tongue in frustration.

"You think I'll chicken out."

"*I think I want to make sure you're in for the good kind of surprise.*"

"Won't it ruin the surprise if you lay out the whole plan for me?" I argue, not sure how I feel about knowing *everything* he has planned.

"*They'll take about an hour to kick in. Maybe a little less. You'll get drowsy, and you'll simply fall asleep. The dose is low enough that it'll just be there to help you stay asleep.*" He can't hide the way his voice hitches with anticipation, and my ribs unclench a little. "*Don't leave your door unlocked. I know where your spare key is. I'll come pick you up and bring you back here again.*"

"I could just drive over before taking them?" It sort of seems like the easier route.

But he just scoffs, the sound disdainful even on speakerphone. "*No. I want to come get you. I like it, Quinn.*"

"Because you're a kidnapper?"

"*Because I said so. I meant what I said. That I want to fuck you while you're asleep. I don't know how long it'll take you to wake up. You might be scared when you do. I'll stop, make sure you're okay, and see what you want to do. But you'll be asleep for a little while. You sure you want to do this?*"

"If you keep asking me, I'm going to say no just to spite you." I don't really mean it. It's the nerves, and the excitement. I take a deep breath, close my eyes, and count to ten before speaking again. "Yes. I really want to do this. I know you won't hurt me."

"*You trust me?*"

"Well, you've literally drugged me once already and kidnapped me twice. So, yeah. At this point, this kind of feels like child's play." It doesn't. How could it ever? But I'm afraid to tell him that.

"*If at any time you say 'red' I'll stop. If I think you aren't enjoying it, I'll stop. You have my word on that.*"

"Thanks," I whisper, meaning to say it louder and failing. "So... an hour and a half?"

"*You have tomorrow off, right?*"

"The whole damn weekend." I pop the cap off of the pill bottle. "And you want me to do this? You're really into it?"

"*More than you could ever know.*"

"Because I'm about to take them."

"*I'll stay on the phone with you while you do.*"

His words are a comfort that I don't expect. I flip the pills into my hand, staring at them, and take a breath. "Now or never," I mutter, tipping them into my mouth. There's a bottle of water beside me that I uncap, and seconds later, the pills have been swallowed.

"Okay, umm. I did it." It's too late now to feel this nervous, or be this shaky. "I'll see you later?"

"*I'll take care of you, Quinn,*" Gabriel purrs, sending shivers down my body. "*Just go to sleep, princess. I promise I'll take care of you.*"

"Just..." I don't know what I want to say, and for a moment I feel nauseous. I'm so nervous, more than I thought I'd be, as I curl up on my side under my blanket. "Promise me it'll be okay?" I hope more than anything that I don't dream of my old home, or of the face that keeps popping into my dreams, only to fade away as soon as I open my eyes before I can properly remember what I'm seeing.

"*It'll be more than okay. Just trust me.*"

"We'll see." I close my eyes and let out a long breath. "Good night, Gabriel."

"*See you soon, Quinn.*"

. . .

THE FIRST THING that my mind focuses on is the heat between my thighs. The next is the way my whole body trembles, muscles aching like I've been working out.

Teeth graze my neck, and Gabriel's warm palm massages my breast as he fucks me. His strokes are slow and relaxed. Easy, like he has all night. And maybe he does.

"Are you really waking up this time, my perfect girl?" he purrs in my ear. "Want to see the wreck I've made of you?"

I can't open my eyes or move, though he isn't holding me down whatsoever. I'm so close to coming that I can barely breathe right, though the ache in my body makes me think this isn't the first time.

"No, I don't think you are. Not yet. Go back to sleep, gorgeous girl. Let me play with you a while longer."

"Gabriel..." The word is slurred and hard to say. The only thing I can do is nuzzle his jaw, his stubble scraping my skin. I murmur his name once more, prompting a soft laugh from him.

"I know, baby. But I'm not done. Go back to sleep for me. Like I said, I want to play with you a while longer." When I try to say something else, he shushes me with a kiss. "Do you want to come first? I bet it'll put you right back out, won't it?"

He moves his hand to my clit, rubbing it with his fingers and drawing a surprised whimper from me. It's sensitive too, like he really has been playing with me for longer than I think. Then again, I have no idea what time it is, or even if it's still storming outside.

All I know is how I feel. How the heat and need build in my body, prompting a soft whine to escape my lips.

His teeth close over my neck, the pain sparking more awareness from me as he picks up the pace. He's saying something, though I don't know what. All I know is that it's easy for him to move me as he wants, my leg going over his shoulder so he can fuck me more deeply.

My release takes me by surprise, my lips parting in a gasp that he catches on his tongue. He's not far behind, and I feel him slam into me one last time, coming inside me as he whispers possessive promises in my ears.

I can barely hear them, though. My consciousness fades as he pulls out, and the last thing my brain registers is the soft sound of satisfaction against my ear and his words as I go out again.

"I'm nowhere near done with you, Quinn."

The next time consciousness finds me, I'm somewhat disappointed that he's not fucking me.

The feeling only lasts a few moments, though. Three fingers press inside me, dragging a moan from my lips that causes Gabriel to pause.

"Is the fourth time the charm, princess?" he goads, thrusting his fingers deep. "I think it should be. I want you to wake up and see what you look like. For you to tell me how you feel."

I writhe under him, feeling sore and completely wrecked. My body is achy, like my muscles have been working overtime, and even him fingering me makes me let out a soft sound of disagreement.

"It's too much," I whimper, trying to open my eyes. They flutter open, then close, and I find I don't have the strength to do it again. "Gabriel—"

"It's been over twenty minutes since you last came, Quinn," he taunts, his thumb stroking over my clit. I try to pull away from him, but he pins me down. With his other hand on my stomach as he slides his fingers free and brushes them lightly against my entrance. "Can you tell me how you feel? Do you want to use the safe word I gave you?"

I have to think about it, and thinking is hard just now. I take a couple of deep breaths and take stock of myself. There's nothing wrong with me. Except that I'm sweaty and exhausted, with a body that feels absolutely wrecked and brought to the edge and back.

But there's nothing *wrong*.

"I'm fine," I say, finally opening my eyes. "I mean, I don't want to use it. Okay?" I look down at him, like it's somehow his decision, and he studies my face for a few moments before his lips curve into a grin.

"Good girl," he praises, his fingers sliding into me again. He adds another, and I nearly choke at the feeling of *four* fingers in my body, pressing deep. "So good for me. You look so good like this, and you're so full of my cum. I thought maybe I'd slide a toy into this pretty pussy, keep you nice and full for me until I'm ready to play with you again. Doesn't that sound perfect?"

The best I can do is whine. Especially with how full his fingers make me feel, and the way my thighs tremble and tense in anticipation. "Fuck me," I mumble, when I can sort out the words. "Please."

"Why?" Gabriel taunts, pressing my knees wider so he can kneel over me. When I crack my eyes open, the first thing I see is his face, and I don't want to look anywhere else.

Maybe it's a testament to how I've always seemed to feel around him that I'm never able to look away. His tousled hair is swept back from his angular face, and his warm brown eyes are intent on mine. The shadow of a beard is more noticeable today. More pronounced, like he forgot to shave or just didn't want to. Is that the rasping, almost burning feeling I can only slightly recall on my thighs?

"Because I said so," I reply, mouth falling into an easy smile.

"Because it'll feel so good when you're sloppy and loose? When you can barely move? You're such a good little toy for me, aren't you? You *love* that I've been using you all night however I want." He pulls his fingers out of me and pushes up one of my knees until it's nearly against my chest. "You're leaking my cum, but you just want more. What a selfish, vicious thing."

When he slides into me, I cry out more sharply than I'd intended. The world snaps into focus, and my head spins at the intensity of the feeling. For me to feel like this just from his cock, he really must have been doing this for the last couple of hours. "Wait," I grit out, one hand trying to find his hair. It's still so hard to focus. So hard to do anything but take whatever he wants. "*Wait.*"

"No," he purrs, and nips lightly at my bruised throat. "No, baby. You told me to fuck you. You were so sure, even though I was being *nice.*" His thrusts are anything but, and I squeeze my eyes closed at how the feeling tips between pleasure and pain. Without me realizing what it is, I feel burning wetness trail down my face, and it isn't until Gabriel's tongue laps up the tears that I realize I'm crying from overstimulation.

"One more," he purrs. "One more, Quinn. I just want you to come one more time for me, okay?"

"Do you promise?" I whine, finally able to hitch my arms around his neck.

"Sure, baby." He fucks me just as languidly as I remember from the last time I woke up. Long, deep thrusts that leave me breathless and dizzy. It doesn't take long, not when every thrust slides over a spot inside of my body that makes me see stars. I'm panting, begging, with my head tipped back so he can mark up my neck and shoulders at his leisure.

My body trembles, arms tightening around his shoulders as I come. It's different from what I'm used to, the pleasure of it mingling with the feeling of my orgasm being wrung from my body. This time I whimper against his neck as he leans over me, clutching him tight as he continues to fuck me to his own completion.

It isn't long. A soft curse lands against my ear, and his hands on my hips tighten, dragging me up to him so he can bury his length in my willing cunt. "You're so good at taking this. So good at letting me play with you," he murmurs against my jaw. Before I can formulate a reply, he's pulled away, sitting up between my thighs and holding my hips to stare down at me.

"What are you doing?" I ask, perplexed and missing him just a little. "Gabriel?"

"Watching my cum leak out of your sweet little pussy," he replies, leaning down to kiss my stomach. I watch him, bemused, and my breath catches in my chest when his tongue licks a stripe up my clit.

"I can't," I say, trying to sit up, but still too dizzy to do it well. "Gabriel—" A hand on my stomach pushes me back down, and his eyes find mine as he licks me again.

"Yeah, you can," he argues, a cruel grin on his face. "Just one more. I know you can for me."

"I really can't," I breathe, air filling my lungs sharply as I feel his fingers at my opening. "Gabriel, *please*—" He isn't listening, or he doesn't believe me. I feel his fingers on my inner thighs, skimming along my skin, before two of them are shoved into my entrance deeply, then pulled out again.

"What are you doing?" I demand, staring at the still-spinning ceiling.

"Putting all of my cum back where it belongs. I've worked

too hard for it to go to waste so soon. And do you know how *hot* you are right now? You can't see yourself, but I'll paint a picture for you. Trembling and fucking ruined in my bed, with my cum leaking out of your cunt. Next time, I'm going to fill up both your holes and I really will keep a toy in you until I'm ready to play again. I want to see you begging and needy, so full you can't walk straight. I want to see you too afraid to get out of bed because you know my cum will trickle down your thighs."

"It won't stay," I whine, my pussy clenching around his fingers again. "Gravity is a fucking thing, and you're just doing that to be mean."

"If I were doing it to be mean, you'd know," he assures me. "But if you're worried about gravity..." He sits up and jerks me into his lap, my hips tilted upward so he can grab a pillow and stuff it under me. "Now I can keep you like this as long as I like. And I think I want to see you cum without my cock this time." His fingers come back, and he leans over me enough that his fingers can tease my too-sensitive body. I shudder under his touch, his fingers relentless as he teases my nipples into stiff peaks once more.

"I can't," I whisper, throwing my head back against the bed. He presses three fingers into me, then another, until I'm nearly sobbing at the feel of them. "I *can't*," I say again, my voice hoarse as more tears run down my face. "Please, I can't—"

"You can, my gorgeous little toy. You can come for me if I want you to. On my fingers, just like this. Let me feel your pussy flutter around my fingers. I know you're tired, but I just want one more."

"But you promised, you said—"

"I lied," he interrupts sharply, picking up the movements of his fingers. "I lied to you. Because I'm just so greedy for this.

You can't blame me when you look like *that*, can you? How was I supposed to keep my word?"

My hips arch weakly into his hands as my muscles tense. Against my will, my thighs are trembling, clenching, and my body fights the arousal and exhaustion. "I really, really can't," I promise, the words too loud and too high. I sound like I'm crying, and maybe I am.

"You really, *really* can. You're so close, Quinn. So *fucking close*. Come on my fingers. You don't have a choice, baby. Come for me." His thumb finds my clit and rubs it harshly, the feeling sending me into a shrieking mess. "Yeah, you fucking love that. I know it's too much, so *fucking come for me*, princess. Right now. Come on my fingers—" He breaks off when I *scream*, my body finally giving up the fight as a last orgasm tears through me.

"Just. Like. That." His fingers thrust into me on every word, and he forces my orgasm to go as long as it can before finally, *finally*, his fingers slide free and he watches me shake myself into a million pieces on the bed.

With my consciousness still trying to piece itself back together and my heart beating out a racing rhythm, I don't expect anything from him except to watch me.

I don't expect him to get up off of the bed, though I barely notice when he walks into his ensuite bathroom. My eyes close hard, and I bury my face in my palm, trying to stop the world from spinning.

More than anything, I don't expect it when he comes back to kneel beside me, pulling my hand from my face so he can murmur comforting praises against my skin and kiss me sweetly on the lips and nose. "Good girl. You were so good for me. Let me take care of you, sweet girl. Perfect Quinn." There's a damp rag in his hand, and he uses it to gently swipe over my skin, cleaning me up from his cum and the sticky sweat that's making me uncomfortably cold.

It doesn't take long, though he doesn't hurry. He never leaves me, his words soft in my ears as he cleans me up and finally helps me sit up, knees braced under me. "Here." He holds out an oversized tee, a crooked smile on his face. "I wasn't sure if you'd want to sleep in anything that fit snugly, so I got you this."

When I don't complain, Gabriel helps me into the shirt, and I find he's right. I don't want to wear anything else.

"What are you going to do?" I ask, getting a good look at him for the first time as he pulls on a pair of lightweight sleep pants. "Are you going to stay?"

"Am I going to stay?" he repeats, kneeling back onto the bed with me. "You couldn't chase me away with a broom." There's something different about him tonight. Something I usually see flashes of, but never full-on moments.

He's acting so sweet. Caring, even. Like he's worried about me.

Like he wants to take care of me.

"Oh," I say, blinking at him like an idiot. "Umm. Good. I want you to stay. I want you to—" I'm cut off when he drags me down under the blankets with him, and the warmth triggers my sleepiness once again.

"You were so good," he says, like he wants me to absorb the meaning into my bones. An arm curls around me, and when he pulls me close, it's just so he can press as much of me as he can against him. "Thank you."

"For what?"

"For giving me this. Did you enjoy it too?"

I think about it as I turn myself over to face him, unsurprised that I can't read his expression in the dark room. The storms have passed, though I'm not sure how long they've been gone, and it's still dark enough that it could be anywhere from three to five am.

"Way more than I thought I would," I admit, snuggling as close to him as I can. "I *suppose* I would be willing to open negotiations to do it again sometime. But mostly because it's the best sleep I've ever had in my life."

He laughs, the sound loud and sudden enough that it seems like I've surprised him. "I would love to hear what your opening negotiations are," he agrees, tucking my head under his chin. "Another day. Go to sleep, sweet girl. I'll take care of you as long as you want me to."

I want to reply with something sharp and witty. To tell him to be careful what he promises, or I'll have him serving me hand and foot for the next decade. But I'm too far gone. Too groggy, and too eager to get back to sleep to do anything more and press my nose against his chest and inhale the dangerous, musky scent I can't get enough of.

TWENTY-ONE

The weather reports hadn't been accurate when they'd mentioned tonight would be one of the worst storms in recent Springwood, IL history. They should've said it was biblical flood proportions instead.

I look up through the trees, my heart beating fast in my chest. It slams against my chest, over and over again, trying to force my ribs to bend and break for it to escape. But I stand my ground, staring up at the dizzying, sleeting rain.

Thunder sounds like a rumble that permeates my body, running up and down my bones as something itches at the back of my neck, setting me on edge.

Turn around.

Turn around, Quinn.

I turn, pivoting on one foot, and my heart jolts upward to lodge in my throat. Billy Owens is just as pissed off as he had been at the party I never should've gone to. Only now, there's no one around to shove a drink into his hand or tell him to chill out, that I'm just that freaky girl with no home and no manners.

There's nothing to do except look at him. My lips parted as rain cascades over my cold, clammy skin. "Go away," I say, my voice torn away by the wind. "Leave me alone." I say the second part louder, though he acts as if he hasn't heard me.

"Go away," I repeat, my words pleading. "Please, I don't want —" He strides forward and grabs my arm, yanking me to him. I'm scrawny for eighteen, and my head barely reaches his shoulder. His fingers encircle my wrist easily, with room to spare, and he grips so tight that I feel the bones in my wrist grinding together.

I cry out and the dream-memory flickers, melting around the edges. There's a flurry of movement around me, and the crack of lightning blinds me against my surroundings just in time for my hand to curl around something cold and slick—

When I look down, Billy is on the ground, his eyes wide and accusatory. There's someone else here, and the object in my hand is a phone, not what it might have been before.

"Help me," I whisper, staring at the figure in the rain. "Please, please help me. I didn't mean to—"

Gabriel reaches out much as Billy had, but he grips my shoulder instead of my bruised wrist. His mouth opens as he watches me with cold, dark eyes, but instead of words, a ringing noise fills my ears.

He speaks again, but another harsh, grating ring finds my ears instead. The rain picks up against my face, but seconds later I'm numb. The dream fades, darkening, but not before I hear Gabriel's voice instead of the ringing phone.

"You'll tell them it was an accident."

I jerk upward from my desk, face burning where it's been pressed awkwardly on the edge of my laptop. The world around me spins, the thunder from my dreams causing my bones to vibrate and my head to spin.

My cell phone rings on my desk, the noise earsplitting and irritating. Though in this case, it saved me from an unfortunate dream, so I guess I should be kind of grateful.

It takes a few moments for me to realize where I am, and

then to appreciate that no one else is in the office while I took my unplanned nap.

The storm outside rages, and I can't remember if the weather channel had said anything about thunder loud enough to shake a small building. The lightning that hits next is brighter than before and causes me to go momentarily blind in the dark office.

Dark.

There should be lights on, but I'm in the near-pitch black. I've missed the call by now, but when I check it and see a number I don't know, I immediately push any concern to the side. Instead, I use my phone as a flashlight, getting up and going to the light switch panel on the wall.

They're all turned on, cementing my belief that the power is off. The only light in the office comes from the windows, and from Melinda's office.

I blink stupidly, wondering if she's on some kind of generator that she keeps from us peasants, and decide that since no one is here, I shouldn't be *that* worried about going into where my boss works.

I need light, after all. Maybe there's something in there to help.

As I walk in, I find her number in my phone and call it. At the very least, I should report a power outage, though I'll have to lie about how long it's been out. I have no way of knowing, though I hope it hasn't been long. Maybe this is just a really long flicker, instead of an actual outage.

The phone rings once, then again as I circle her desk to look for the source of the light, though it goes off as soon as I start to really look for it. Another ring echoes through the office when I put my phone on speaker, my hand traveling to her desk and all the files on top of it. When did she get this unorganized? Normally when I'm in here, Melinda is the epitome of tidiness.

"*This is Melinda Wilkes; please leave a message. If you need the social services office, please call...*" her voice trails off as she cites the office number, and for a moment, I consider leaving a message. Until it comes time, and I chicken out, hanging up instead. She'll know I called, and I can just text her if I want to, instead of talking to her about the outage.

You should've left a message, I berate myself, knowing it'll look suspicious when I call back and do it. A text feels like the wrong choice here. If I call again, maybe she'll know it's urgent and actually pick up.

My fingers close around an old flip phone just as her voicemail triggers again, inviting me to leave a message or call the office where I'm currently standing.

"Hey, Melinda," I say, then pause to let a peal of thunder stop echoing throughout the room. "I'm at the office and, umm. Could you give me a call? The electric—" My phone vibrates to alert me to another call coming in, and I move it so I can see the screen, half-expecting it to be my boss calling while I'm leaving a message.

Instead, it's the same unknown number as before.

"The power is out," I say, continuing my message to Melinda as I wonder if I want to pick up the call. "It's been out for a bit, and I didn't know if there was something I should do. Somewhere I should call?" The other call cuts out, signaling it's gone to my voicemail.

"Call me back. I'll be here for a few minutes, but I'm probably going to lock up and go home since there's no power." It's already ten, and with no one coming in until Monday, I'm the last one in the office all weekend. If Melinda doesn't come check on things, it'll be days until we know if the power is back on.

But checking the power, or staying any longer, is way above my pay grade. My night now consists of figuring out if the storm is bad enough that I won't be able to make it home safely.

Hanging up, I glance at the flip phone in my hand. It's battered and dull silver, like something out of the early 2010s. I haven't seen a phone like this in years. I look it over, knowing I should leave it alone. It isn't mine, after all. I don't have any right to go through Melinda's things. Or at least what's on her desk.

Absently, my eyes flick back to my phone, looking at the two calls from the same local number. I *am* the one on call, and it's not unheard of for my colleagues to get calls on their cell phones. Especially if this is Melinda's husband, or her calling from another phone.

With that thought in mind, I call the number back, half-expecting it to go to voicemail.

Instead, my call is picked up on the second ring, and my ears are assaulted by the sound of panting, frantic breaths. *"Make her stop,"* Mr. Durham snarls in my ear. *"I did what you said. Make her stop."*

The words send a jolt of surprise up my spine and I look at my phone as if it can give me the answer to what the hell is going on, just as the other phone in my hand lights up with a message.

"Make who stop?" I ask, my voice soft. "Where are you?"

"It's because I mentioned the Birkins, isn't it? Tell her I won't tell anyone—" he breaks off with a curse, and it sounds as if he's running or tripping through the underbrush.

"Where are you?" I ask, thoughts spinning. Flipping open the old phone, I look at the cracked screen and press the button to read the message. I have no right doing this. None at all. But now I can't help myself.

"*The woods of Ridgeback Marina. Tell her whatever you need in order to get her to stop. Whatever you want me to do—*" he breaks off again, and I swear I hear a woman's voice from somewhere much further away, though I can't make out the exact tone or what's said. "*Help me!*" he hisses, then the call is dropped

I wouldn't know what to say, anyway. I'm too busy staring at the message on the other phone, which causes my stomach to twist into knots.

Get rid of her.

Now I'm starting to think this phone *isn't* my boss's. The words are ominous, sent from a number that's not saved in the phone. Though when I check the address book, I find there are no saved numbers at all.

"Shit," I mutter, pocketing the phone and back out of the room. Is my boss in danger? Is she at the marina, and the calls I'm getting from Mr. Durham are connected to whatever this message is? That's definitely a stretch, but with the way my dream has me worked up and everything that's happened in the last ten minutes, I'm willing to go out on this limb.

As I put my phone to my ear again, I let out a breath when the person I've called picks up after one ring. "Hi," I say, my shoulders dropping as some of the tension in them eases. At least he's fine, and I haven't gone to voicemail. Though in reality, Gabriel is the person whose safety I need to worry about the least.

"*Are you finally off work?*" he drawls, the sound of his tv in the background coming in on every third word. "*Do you want to come over?*"

"The power's out," I say, my words leaving me in a panicked jumble as I grab my jacket and my keys before heading for the door. "I don't know what's going on. Mr. Durham called, and I found this phone—"

"*Quinn—*"

"I'm worried that my boss is in trouble. I don't know, something's wrong. And I've been dreaming, but it's worse now. I didn't tell you before; sometimes I barely remember." I'm rambling as I jog to my car, and when I'm finally in with cool air blasting me in the face, I shiver in all of my rain-soaked glory.

"I always mean to tell you. Well, sort of. It's my thing, and I need to figure out—"

"*What are you dreaming about?*"

"Billy," I say, the word falling like a missile between us.

He's quiet at first. The noise of his television is the only thing I hear apart from the sound of my car's engine and the windshield wipers that squeak against the window.

"*I think you should come over,*" he says at last, his voice oh so careful and controlled. "*I think we should talk about this. We'll figure out where Melinda is, and why Mr. Durham is calling.*"

"I don't think I need to," I argue, eyes narrowed. "I'm going to go find him. Them. I have this phone. I think she's in trouble, and—"

"*Do you know what you sound like right now? Do you know who it feels like I'm talking to?*" Gabriel snaps, his patience evaporating. "*We're not in Springwood, Quinn. Things don't work the same here.*" Is there a touch of worry in his voice? Concern for me? Though I don't know why.

"I don't know what you mean." I close my eyes hard, as the events of my dream run through my head. My other hand closes hard on what I'm holding, and I let out a long, even breath. "I'm fine."

"*You sound like the girl who called me five years ago. The one who just stabbed the town's favorite college athlete.*" A door slams, and I can hear rain on his side of the phone as I stare at the ground in front of me, lit up by my headlights.

"Don't," I whisper, feeling frozen. "Don't you fucking dare—"

"*Then don't move. Don't go anywhere. Let me come find you first, Quinn. Don't do whatever it is you're trying to do.*"

"I'm just going to help. I want to find my boss and Mr. Durham. It's not my case. I know it's technically my boss's, but what if they need help?" My grip flexes around the coolness a the handle, and I look down in surprise at the knife I'm holding in my lap.

Where did this come from?

It's the knife from the break room, but I'm not sure I remember going to get it. *Do I?*

"*You're not in a place to help. Not alone. Just stay in that parking lot, Quinn. Let me come get you so I can help.*"

"It's selfish of me to always ask for your help when things get bloody," I mutter, not pushing away the memory of what he'd looked like that night when he'd stood in the diner.

He'd killed them.

He'd killed Billy's parents for me, and posed their son's body in the diner for the cops to assume was a part of the crime.

But he hadn't been.

"*It's what I'm here for. I'll find you even if you hang up on me, you know.*" God, I need to get the tracker out of my car. I can't be this easy for him to find all the time.

"Yeah," I sigh, leaning back as I lay the knife in the passenger seat and shove the car into gear. "I know."

CHAPTER

TWENTY-TWO

I don't know what's wrong with me.

Something has to be, because now that the dreams of Billy Owens have started, I can't push the memories out of my mind.

I killed him.

My hands tighten on the steering wheel as I drag in deep breaths. For weeks now, I've known I can't keep going like this without something changing. My dreams have been getting worse, and though I haven't wanted to admit that to anyone, even myself, I can't help but wonder if this could have been prevented if I'd just taken things more slowly.

If I'd listened to my body, my brain, and my dreams, would I be here now? Half-frenzied and panicking as I try not to drive off the road?

I take a deep breath and fight back the nausea that's clawing at my throat, unable to close my eyes while I'm driving through the pouring rain. It's impossible not to let the thoughts take over, to expand from the locked box in the back of my brain that I've been keeping them in for so long.

I killed Billy Owens.

I stabbed him with a knife I'd taken from the party, because I was afraid of him when he'd grabbed my wrists and asked why I was leaving so soon. Later, I'd wondered if he was just teasing. Just playing and being over the top, like so many of his friends always accused him of being.

Sometimes you just have to make him believe you really don't want it, I remember a girl telling me before that night. *He just has a hard time hearing what you're saying when he's drunk.* It isn't an excuse. Or if it is, it's a poor one. But I can't help but wonder if I could've ended the night without the blood and death of him and his parents.

They would've had me absolutely crucified. I'd known that the moment Billy had died and I'd been standing over him covered in his blood. I'd sobbed on the phone to my therapist, the one person in life who had given me a chance and actually sat down to listen to me.

Are you sorry you killed him? The words echoed around between my ears when Gabriel had asked them, standing on the other side of Billy's body in the park.

I'd been a lot more honest with myself, and with him, back then. I'd looked into his face and instead of saying the right thing. Instead of lying and telling him how bad I felt, I just shook my head, opened my mouth, and told him *no.*

I hadn't felt bad for Billy at all.

I'd only been upset for myself.

Gabriel had offered to help. Had told me that he'd take care of it. He'd convinced me to go home and wait, but I hadn't done that. I'd gone to the diner, for some reason. To apologize. To tell them what I'd done.

To kill them too? The thought is an unpleasant one, and my stomach twists harshly. It's easy to think I'm sane enough to *not* have wanted to kill Billy's parents just to try to circumvent them finding out what I'd done.

It's easy to think that now, when I'm feeling only an echo of what I'd felt that night.

I saw a girl planning a murder.

That's what Gabriel said to me, but he'd been talking about when we'd first met. When I'd been the angry, abused foster kid with no one to talk to.

But had he meant it about that night as well?

Would I have killed them?

"Stop." My voice is loud in my car, even though it competes with the pounding rain. "*Stop*, Quinn." It was too long ago. Too far in the past for me to have an existential crisis in my car today instead of all those years ago. If I've lived with myself this long, I'm sure as hell going to make it for another eighty years.

The sign for Ridgeback Marina comes into view, lit up by my brights on the empty, rural road. This late at night and in this weather, I haven't passed a single soul. Even when I slow down and make my way into the parking lot of the marina, that's surrounded by forest, I don't see anyone else.

Except for two cars, anyway. One of them I don't recognize, but the other makes my breath catch in my throat. It's Melinda's car, and my worry for her cements in my chest. Is someone trying to kill my boss? I'd thought Mr. Durham was in distress when he'd called me, but maybe that's what he'd wanted me to think. I've heard the rare story of a person getting mad or violent with their case worker when things aren't going their way.

Is that what's happening here? Mr. Durham is technically one of Melinda's cases, just like the Birkins were. One she'd started putting off in the same way she had them. Maybe she's getting lax, complacent, or lazy enough for her clients to start despising her and wanting revenge.

It wouldn't be more fucked up than other things I've witnessed in my life.

I park on the other side of Melinda's car, needing a moment to calm myself down. I press myself against the seat, flush with it and tilting my head back against the headrest. With my eyes closed, I watch the lightning from behind my lids and suck in a few breaths.

If I'm going to be here doing something stupid, the least I can do is not do it while panicking.

When I open my eyes and look out my window, I nearly die on the spot. A soft shriek leaves my lips, followed by a hysterical giggle as Gabriel, looking like a drowned, pissed off cat, stares at me. I clap a hand to my mouth as I giggle at his appearance once again.

He doesn't wait for me to figure him out, though. Gabriel yanks open the door of the car, taking advantage of it being unlocked, unbuckles my seatbelt, and drags me out into the rain. Thankfully, from what I can tell, the rain is starting to lessen. At least, it doesn't seem as bad as it had been while I'd been driving here from the middle of town.

"You're reckless!" he snaps, grabbing my upper arms. "What are you even *doing* out here?" His eyes catch on something as he looks past me into the car, and I know what he sees.

"I didn't mean to bring it, I don't think," I admit, my voice barely loud enough to be heard over the rain.

"Yes, you did." He leans past me and grabs the knife, jamming it into his jeans and covering it with his shirt and jacket. Gabriel glares down at me, though I can see a hint of amusement behind the exasperation on his face. "You're a monster," he tells me, not letting go.

"Sorry?"

"I just wish you'd *listen* to me once in a while." He leans forward, and my body tenses, ready for whatever he's planning on doing. Gabriel is irritated at best. Frustrated, angry even, at worst. If he wants to throw me over his shoulder and put me in his trunk, there's not a lot I can do about it.

I'm not expecting him to kiss me. His wet mouth slides, slick against mine, and I wrap an arm around his shoulders to pull him down for a quick, filthy kiss.

It's him that pulls away first, brows raised. The rain is definitely letting up now, though both of us are soaked and I can feel the rain trickling down my scalp uncomfortably.

"Well, let's go then," he sighs, shoving his wet hair back from his face. From his other pocket comes a small flashlight, and I see the flash of something metallic against his skin.

Does he have a weapon other than my stolen knife?

"I don't even know where we're going," I admit, putting my phone to my ear as I try Melinda for a third time. She doesn't pick up, not that I expect her to, and I follow him toward the marina, where he's walking with a purpose in mind.

"Call your boss," he orders over the rain. "See if she's here."

"I just did," I argue, catching up to him and pointing at her car. "She's here somewhere. And Mr. Durham has to be as well. I think he's going to hurt her!" I lift my voice to be heard over the thunder, needing to lengthen my stride and nearly jog to keep up with him.

But he barely seems to notice. He looks around constantly, as if worried about what we're going into. As if there's something more to be worried about than what I've counted on.

And really, he's the expert, isn't he? If someone is going to know what to worry about, it's him.

The marina shop is locked, and the only lights on inside are the ones from a vending machine that cast a blue light over the inside of the building. The rain continues, sounding against the tin roof above us as I walk away from the building to the dock instead.

The lake is creepy in the dark, in the rain. I look out across it with my hands shoved into my pockets as if that can cut the snapping cold that's bringing the occasional shiver down my spine. Boats rock in their spots, bumping lightly against the dock as the water churns and the wind blows white caps into existence.

"Fuck," I murmur, unable to *not* think about how questionable this whole trip is. "I'm really not looking to solve a murder case," I admit as Gabriel stops on the dock beside me. "I don't feel very Scooby-gang, if I'm being honest."

"Me neither," he shrugs. "But I'm not the one with the mysterious phone, a knife, and a guy calling you who may or may not be a murderer. Come on." He walks away from me, heading for the woods nearest the marina. I follow. It's a good idea, since this is where I've gotten called from tonight. But still, a chill crawls up my spine that has nothing to do with the rain.

Gabriel, however, stops at the edge of the woods to turn and raise a brow. He gestures onward, as if in invitation, and I stop beside him, my own eyes wide in surprise at his movements. "What?" I ask, not needing to talk so loudly here. "What's wrong?"

"Nothing," he assures me. "I'm not the one doing stupid shit. You're the savior of the day, so *you* lead."

"Then give me my knife," I reply, crossing my arms over my chest and trying not to look like I'm shivering. "So I can defend myself if I need to."

He eyes me up and down thoughtfully, meeting my eyes before speaking. "I don't know," he says at last. "I can protect you, you know."

"I can protect myself!" I snap back, holding my hand out for the weapon. "That's why I brought the damn knife."

He hands it to me without another word, though I swear I see the hint of a grin on his lips as the darkness of his eyes deepens.

Does he *want* me to have the knife? Was there some point in making me demand it, instead of just letting me keep it from the start?

I meet his gaze as I tuck it into my sleeve. The cuffs of my hoodie are tight enough that I can easily keep it there, though once it's there and I'm walking down the small trail that winds through the woods, I realize that I have another problem.

I have no idea what I'm doing or where I should go. I try Melinda again on my phone, frowning at the ground as I look around me for signs of something. A struggle, maybe? Or a sign painted in blood to show me where to go?

Melinda doesn't pick up, and neither does Mr. Durham. Gabriel follows me, his off-key whistling the soundtrack to my night. Too bad he's not more help than that. Every time I look back at him, all I get is a baleful stare in reply.

"You're no help," I say finally, stomping up a small incline. "Literally none at all."

"What would you like me to do, exactly?" he drawls, fingers catching at my hood just long enough to make me notice. "I have no idea where you're trying to go. I don't know this place, Quinn."

"If it were me that was lost, and you thought I was about to die, would you do more?" I ask in irritation, wishing he could give me an idea of how to track people down in the rain at night.

"No."

The word brings me to a quick halt, stopping so fast that he nearly runs into me. My heart stutters in my chest at the unexpected answer, and I look up at him in surprise when he prowls around to stand at my side, trying not to look absolutely devastated.

"No," he says again, pushing my wet hair back from my face. "Because I'd never let you get so far that I would have to worry." He cups my cheek in his large hand, melting some of the cold that's frozen me to the core. "I'll always protect you, Quinn," he purrs, face close to mine. "Even if that means tossing you in my trunk if you ever try to do stupid shit like this again."

"That sounds uncomfortable," I admit, distracted from my current problems.

"Very," he agrees. "So behave."

Before I can reply, a scream breaks through the storm. I pull away from him, eyes scanning the darkness of the woods as I tighten my fingers around my too-long sleeve that hides my knife. Movement finally draws my attention, and I take a few steps forward as Mr. Durham sprints toward me, tripping and falling flat on his face on the trail before pushing himself back to his feet, clothes covered in mud.

"Well, that's... not what I was expecting," Gabriel admits at my side. "Are you sure you know what's going on here?"

I shake my head, eyes narrowed. Durham sees me a second later and reaches out to me like I'm going to take his hand and yank him free of the situation. I don't, however. I let him come to me until Gabriel steps between us and puts a warning hand up against his chest to stop Durham from crashing into me.

"Did you tell her?" he huffs, reaching out and snagging the edge of Gabriel's jacket. "She's still following me. She won't *stop*. Just tell her I won't tell anyone. I'm just trying to get my son back." He turns pleading eyes on Gabriel. "You understand me. You know I'll do whatever I need to. No more drinking or violence. No more talking about things I don't know, I *swear*."

"I'm... confused," I admit, drawing his attention back to me. "Mr. Durham." I blink and shove my hair away from my face. "What's going on here?" I don't want to say that I'd expected *him* to be the danger, not the one *in* danger. "Who are you afraid of?"

He stares at me, surprise warring with disbelief on his thin face. "You're joking," he whispers finally. "Tell me you're joking."

I shake my head and shrug. "No jokes here. I don't know what's going on."

"I thought you'd come here to help me. I thought that was the point of this." He looks behind him and around us, searching for someone that isn't here. "I thought you were telling her to stop." I can see him getting angry, getting upset. His face reddens and when he whirls on me again, there's hate in his dark eyes. "You stupid bitch. What are you doing here if you aren't here to tell her to fucking stop?"

"Telling *who* to stop *what?*" I snap, losing my patience and a little flabbergasted at the sudden change in his demeanor. "Mr. Durham, tell us what's going on so that we can actually *help you*, instead of standing here in the rain."

He sucks in a breath, then another. I see him trying to calm down, just as well as I can see that it's barely working. He's furious with *me*, though I haven't done anything wrong. "I want your help. I thought you understood. You talked to me, and you didn't seem mad like she is. I thought that's why you were on my case now, because I'm not in trouble anymore."

"*Who?*" I demand, stepping forward to grab his jacket and shake him by it. "What's going on? Who are you running from?"

"Your boss!" he yells, loudly enough that his voice echoes. "Let go, damn it! If you're not here to help me, then I need to get away from here."

"My *boss*? Why is she chasing you?" I repeat. My head is spinning, and I can see Gabriel shifting from the corner of my eye, like something has occurred to him and makes him uncomfortable with the situation at hand.

Like he knows something I don't.

"Quinn, why don't you step back?" he murmurs in my ear, moving to grip my shoulder. "Step back *now*."

"Why?" I demand, turning to look at him. "What's going on here?"

"Why don't you ask your boss and find out?" Drawing my attention with the words, he waits for me to look at him and points up the trail, where a woman in a rain jacket is striding down the path like she comes here all the time.

There's a smile on Melinda's face that reminds me of the first time I'd met her. All kindness and understanding, without a bit of impatience. The rain doesn't seem to bother her, from what I can tell. But then again, the thing that I can't stop fixating on is the gun in her gloved hand that she holds with a comfortable ease.

"What a surprise, seeing you out here," my boss greets when she's only ten feet away from us. "I thought the weather would be bad enough to keep everyone away. Do you two come here often?"

CHAPTER

TWENTY-THREE

"Do we... come here often?" I repeat, a little confused. "Is that what you just asked?"

Melinda nods, the gun still held at her side in a relaxed grip. "My husband and I come here quite a bit. We like the trails and watching the boats. No boats tonight, of course. But I could see the appeal if the two of you are going off on a secret, clandestine hike." She wiggles her brows at the two of us, and it only deepens my confusion.

"Us?" I repeat, gesturing first at myself, then at Gabriel. I'm not afraid of her like I should be, and like Durham clearly is, as he grips my arm and looks like he's searching for a way to escape. "Like, you mean *us*?"

"The two of you are dreadful at keeping your feelings hidden. I've known for weeks. Don't worry, Quinn. I'm not about to discipline you for your distinguished gentlemen friend," she chuckles, waving her free hand at me.

Something has to be missing. My fear, for one. I've never been afraid of my boss in my life. She's so unthreatening that the idea of it seems ridiculous. Not to mention I still have no clue what's going on here.

"Mr. Durham called me," I admit, pointing at Durham. "He told me... well, I don't know what he told me. He was kind of frantic, umm..." I look at him, then back at Melinda. "Can you explain to me what's going on? I found a phone on your desk. I thought you were in danger, actually. Are you, maybe, not in danger?"

"I don't think she's in danger," Gabriel admits from my other side. "Not in the least."

"Yeah, I'm starting to get that," I mutter back.

"Did I leave my phone?" Melinda pats the pockets of her jacket, looking distressed. When I hold my hand up with the old flip phone in it, however, realization dawns on her face. "It was in the finished case pile, wasn't it? I laid it there when Clara came to talk to me. That's so sweet of you to worry about me. I'm sorry you had to come all this way." She lifts the gun suddenly, and cocks it, just as Durham darts behind me to use me as a human shield.

Gabriel's reaction is instant. He moves to stand in front of me, gripping my arm, and meets Melinda's eyes with a shake of his head. "Don't," he states, and she only frowns in irritation at him, her features drawn on her pale, moon-shaped face.

"I wouldn't shoot Quinn," she informs him. "Once he's dead, we can chat about this. See if we can come to an understanding. I should think this is nothing new to you, Dr. Brooks." When he doesn't reply, she goes on. "You're quite famous in some circles. We're not *that* far from Springwood, after all."

"You have a fan," I mutter, earning the ire of his glare. I roll my eyes when his irritation deepens, and I move to grab Durham's arm to jerk him out from behind me. "Why is she trying to kill you?" I snap, hoping to God that she's telling the truth and not going to shoot me or Gabriel.

He doesn't answer. He's too busy trying to get away from me, and I drag him to the ground, pinning him there with one knee. "Tell me!" I snap, feeling wired. "Why does she want to *shoot you*, Mr. Durham? What did you do?"

"I didn't do anything!" he yells, frantic in his words and his attempts to get away from me. I hear the gun safety clicked back on, and Melinda appears near me, gazing down at him with contempt. Gabriel isn't far either, and I see the glimmer of metal in his hand as he watches Melinda, seemingly uncaring for what Mr. Durham has to say. "I did what you asked," he goes on, eyes rolling wildly to find Melinda above him. "I've stopped drinking. Worked to get better at everything else. I did what you said, so that I can get my son back."

"Well, that's not precisely true." Melinda kneels down, wincing, and I wonder if she'll be able to get back up. "I *told* you to stop, didn't I? Stop *trying*. I told you that your son wouldn't be coming back to you, no matter what the courts said. I told you that I would transfer you case workers, and you'd just stay on the path you were on. But that's not what you did, is it? The moment the case wasn't on my desk anymore, you sauntered in and threatened my employee. You're lucky he didn't kill you." She nods at Gabriel, then meets my wide, surprised gaze.

"How did you—"

"Security cameras, Quinn dear. They're all over the building, inside and out. Don't worry. I respect your privacy. When things with Mr. Durham wrapped up, I stopped watching." My face burns with embarrassment when I realize what she means, but she isn't done speaking. "So then you tried to win her sympathy. You told her about Ashwick to see what she knew about the murders. You tried to get her thinking. Was your plan to turn her against me?"

"No!" He fights desperately under me, but I'm stronger than him when he's so worn out. "I just want my son back. Please, I promise I'll do better this time. I'll do whatever you say. Whatever you want. I just want *my son.*"

"Then let me cut off the hand you hurt him with," Melinda agrees enthusiastically, like she's on board with the plan.

"Cut off his—" I break off, swallowing the word. She wants to *cut off his hand?* Surely that's a joke.

"You're crazy," Durham hisses, renewing his efforts. "You crazy, fucked up bitch!" He suddenly breaks free, throwing me into Gabriel as he gets to his feet and lunges forward. I expect him to run. I expect him to try to escape, so when he instead tackles Melinda and sends her to her back on the trail, I'm surprised.

I don't stop to think. I lurch forward and with Gabriel's help, I drag him back, kicking and screaming, so that Melinda can get to her feet and dust off her jeans. The disgust and dismissal in her eyes are easily visible, and she looks at us with a tight smile.

"I'm sorry to drag you into this," she tells both of us, looking around for the gun that should be on the ground. "It wasn't my intention—"

The gun clicks and I look down, realizing that it's in Durham's hand. There's a desperate light in his eyes as he looks at me, along with an apologetic, grimacing grin. "I can't help it," he says, the words for me as time seems to slow around us. "She doesn't get that I just can't help it. I love my son, but I just get *so angry.* I just need a chance to say I'm sorry. He'll understand." His arm comes up slowly, the gun pointing at my boss.

"He'll love me again. I just need him to have a chance."

The muscles in his arm clench, and I know in a second he's going to shoot. He's too close to miss, and by the resigned look on Melinda's face, she knows it too.

But somehow, as if I've been expecting this, my knife is already in my hand and free from my sleeve. I plunge it into the space between his neck and shoulder, causing him to let out a grunt of surprise as his body jolts where he's pressed against me.

His movements are slow as he looks at me, the gun dropping a few inches before moving in my direction. Blood spurts as he shifts, and another jolt coupled with a soft exhalation of breath is my only indicator that he's been hurt again, until Gabriel pulls away and comes back to slam his metal claws through Durham's throat.

Blood sprays on my face as he removes them, and Durham just... gurgles. The gun falls, clattering to the floor, and he just seems to sit down. There's no death rattle. No climactic last declaration of future vengeance.

He just sits down, then falls onto his back. His eyes never close as the blood pours out of him, and after a few dizzying moments of my heart pounding in my ears and my hands half up, shaking in the empty air, he's done. Breath no longer moves his chest up and down. The blood bubbling at his lips comes to a stop, and his eyes turn glassy.

He's *dead.*

"Hell's bells," Melinda announces, the first one to break the silence. "What a nuisance. Had to be a problem to the very end, didn't he?" She bustles around with Gabriel watching, though I can't stop staring at the dead body in front of me. "Could I have my other phone, Quinn?" she asks, her hand out in front of me. Numbly, I hand it to her, eyes still fixed on his.

"I'm so sorry you two had to be a part of this." She gently wipes off my hands and pushes my sleeves back to my elbows, searching my skin for blood. It's almost motherly, the way she helps me clean up, and I finally blink up at her in absolute surprise.

"You were going to kill him?" I ask, still not able to wrap my head around everything. "Why?"

"Because he was on the road to getting his son back," she replies, her words sour. "Our justice system is imperfect, Quinn." She rips the blade free of his neck and looks up at Gabriel. "You'll keep yours, I assume?"

He nods, flexing the fingers of his clawed glove. "I know how to clean up," he assures her, and the two share a moment, like they're cut from the same cloth.

Hell, maybe they are.

"He hurt his son. Badly. Not to mention his son is terrified of him. It would've ended poorly. I've learned that from experience. I warned him. Over and over again, I told him to stop. He knew what happened to the Birkins when they tried to push getting custody back after what they did. He knew the same thing would happen to him. I *warned* him." She shakes her head at his body and I straighten, arms wrapped around myself, since I don't know where to put them.

"You've killed people before. And you sent me there to find their bodies," I assume quietly. "Why?"

"I needed our county to find them. The police and I have an understanding. No one in this county will stand child abusers for long."

"Why was there a message on the phone on your desk? I thought it was a threat against you. I thought it was *him*," I admit, nodding at the body between us.

"That's my husband," she laughs. "He helps me with cleanup if I need it. Or fixing a scene for the cops." Finally she stands, a plastic bag at her side containing the gun and my knife. "He'll be out here soon," she adds, looking away from

Mr. Durham like he's just a pile of trash. "Are you all right, Quinn? You look like you're in shock. I know killing someone is hard. Everyone's first time is difficult. But he deserved it. The world is a better place for what you did, and I'm fairly grateful to you myself."

"It's not my first," I murmur, unable to stop myself. "I need to go home." I take a few steps back, unwilling to look at either of them. "I just need to go. I won't tell anyone. I'm not." Then I bite my lip and take a breath. "I'm not upset or about to spill your secrets. Okay?" I ask, looking up at my boss and trying to maintain my last bit of self-control as my heart pounds a sharp beat in my ears that shakes my entire being.

"I know you won't. But are you sure you're alright, Quinn?" She trades a look with Gabriel, who's been eyeing me silently for over a minute. "Whatever it is, you can talk to us."

Us. My murdering therapist boyfriend and my murderous boss. I shake my head, the movements sharp. "I just need to go," I say again, taking a few steps back. "I'll be fine. I'll see you... soon."

"This Sunday?" Melinda is quick to suggest. "The husband and I are having a pool party. It's taken us long enough. This Sunday, one to six. Stop by for the pool, stay for the food. Can we count you both in?"

I don't understand what she's asking. Or rather, how in the hell she's asking it. She's talking about a *pool party* while we're standing over a dead body.

I just nod a few times and smile tightly at both of them. "Sunday," I agree, but it's the only thing I can manage before my feet are taking me away, back down the trail, and toward the open parking lot. I try not to break into a run, but it's nearly impossible.

Especially when I hear my name on Gabriel's lips the moment I hit the pavement. I sprint toward my car, trying to get to it before he can catch me, only to be caught and shoved into the side of Melinda's SUV instead.

"Quinn!" Gabriel snaps, searching my face as I cover my mouth with my hands. "Quinn, stop. Talk to me. Tell me what's going on in your head and how I can help."

"*Help?*" I half laugh, half-sob. "You want to *help me?*"

He nods once, then again, more slowly as he takes in my expression. "Just tell me what's going on, okay? Let me help you."

"I don't think you can," I whisper from behind my fingers. "I really don't think you can."

"Why's that, my darling girl?" he murmurs, trapping me against the SUV, his body a line of solid warmth as his arms bracket me in. "Because you're afraid?"

I shake my head.

"Then tell me what's going on."

"I'm terrified," I admit, finally dragging my hands away from my mouth. "I'm so, so *fucking terrified*. Scared is such an understatement."

"Of killing someone."

"No." I take a breath and press my head back against the car. "Because of how much I fucking enjoyed it."

TWENTY-FOUR

H e stares at me as I gasp for air on the side of Melinda's SUV. I can't tell what he's thinking behind his calculating expression. I couldn't even begin to guess, which doesn't happen as often anymore.

One hand trails up my arm to cup my jaw in his long fingers. He teases his thumb over my bottom lip, and finally a soft smile breaks across his mouth. "My little monster," he purrs finally, the sound sending heat straight to my core. "My vicious, darling girl. Can you drive?"

I nod once. It had been my intention, after all.

"Get in your car and drive to my house, as long as you feel safe doing so. You're not light-headed or nauseous?"

I shake my head slowly, eyes narrowing. "You're going home, right?"

"In a minute." He glances back toward the woods, where Durham's body is. "I just want to make sure your boss can handle everything. Do as I say, won't you?" He slips a key between my fingers, pushing it against my palm.

I could *not*. I could just go to my own house, shower, and go to sleep.

But I don't want to. Resisting the pull to him that feels like a constant magnet dragging me into Gabriel's orbit is difficult. Impossible, even, for all the times I've secretly wished him dead.

In fact, it seems like I've hated him for so long that I can't even tell when that hate became something else that's just as searing and intense, with a different four-letter name.

Shit.

"Okay," I say, leaning up on my toes for another kiss. He evades me, smirking as he does, and pulls just out of reach when I try again, only to lean close so he can nip my bottom lip. "Go home. Take a shower. Whatever you need to do, Quinn. I'll be there soon, I swear."

He makes a good argument just by using his mouth to tease mine. I nod and lean back, allowing him to disentangle himself from me so he can step away. "I won't be long," he promises, and gestures to my car.

I give him a mocking, two-fingered salute and walk quickly to my car, getting inside and turning on the engine while he saunters into the woods once more.

When I get into his house, the first thing I do is look around. I haven't been here enough to get the full layout. Plus, if he's going to get mad about it, I'd rather do it when I'm covered in blood and look somewhat scary.

Or sexy, depending on the audience.

I poke around the three-bedroom house with curiosity, finding that the other two upstairs bedrooms are vacant and one is home to a few boxes, the second has nothing at all. The other bathroom, too, looks unused. Though his ensuite is packed with things from body washes to shaving cream, and outfitted with a shower with a head that can be taken off the wall to reach those hard to get places.

Though my only experience with those is from porn I'd watched to get me through college all-night study sessions in my dorm.

A shower is non-negotiable. The blood that's dried on my face and chest is gross and sticky. It's hardening like paint and no matter how much I might enjoy looking at it in the mirror as my heart speeds up at the memory of killing Mr. Durham, it's getting uncomfortable.

He'd deserved it, I tell myself, as if my brain needs a reason. I step into the shower, feeling guilty for *not* feeling guilty, and talk myself into the explanation I barely need.

He hurt his son. Over and over again, I remind myself firmly as the hot water sprays against my chest and face. He'd done more than hurt him. I've seen the files. The reports.

The pictures.

He'd done terrible things to his son, and I'd been stupid for thinking he regretted it when he'd come into my office and been nicer to me. I remember thinking he was there because he cared and was remorseful. Not because he was trying to get away from Melinda's threats.

Then I can't help but wonder how many people she's killed. As the blood from my body stains the water in the shower, I stare at it in the dim light from the bedroom. I hadn't turned on the bathroom lights, not yet, and I can barely see the hint of red in the dirty water that swirls around my feet and disappears down the drain.

While I stare, I take my time. I wash my hair with slow, deliberate touches and work Gabriel's conditioner through it slowly. The blood is well and truly gone by the time I'm done, but I run a washcloth over my skin anyway, half-wishing Gabriel was here to see the blood before it disappears.

I hope he's all right, and that Melinda hasn't ended him too. Though, to be fair, I doubt she could take him on if he really wanted to leave.

Finally, when I have no more reason to stay in the still-hot shower, I turn off the water and step out onto the towel on the tile floor. Shivering in the cold air that flits across my skin, I grab one of his oversized, extra-fluffy towels and wrap it around my body so that I can clear the steamy mirror with one hand.

I look... normal. With no blood and no mud on my skin, I look just like I did this morning. Normal Quinn Riley, with her normal job in Eddyville, Kentucky.

I don't look like someone who just killed a man and enjoyed every second of it.

My fingers clench around nothing, trying to remember how it felt to have the knife in my hand. It had felt so good to fight the resistance of Durham's flesh. To plunge it into his throat as far as it would go.

Would it have felt just as good with Gabriel's claws? If I'd slit his throat instead of stabbing him, would I have gotten the same enjoyment?

When I pick up my clothes, intending to put them back on, I pause with a frown on my lips. They're full of mud and dirt, and enough blood stains them in ways that make me worry I'll have to throw them away. I don't have enough money to keep replacing clothes, that's for sure. But I can't just walk around town with blood all over me, either.

I drop them back to the bathroom floor when I decide not to put them back on, and wrap the towel around me more securely. It's not perfect, but it's something. And I'm just looking for *something* right now until Gabriel gets home and I can hopefully borrow something of his.

With a sigh I flop over onto his bed, groaning my exhaus-

VICIOUS

tion and how much I love the comfort of his mattress. It's sure as hell better than the one I have, and I'm going to make the most of it while I wait.

Knowing he'll wake me up when he gets home, I curl up in Gabriel's bed, drag the blankets over myself, and barely manage to take a deep breath of his scent that lingers in his pillows before I'm completely asleep.

Instead of dreams, the feelings that rush through me drag me out of a comfortable, cool blackness. Dreamless sleep has been a stranger to me lately, so I try as hard as I can to hold on to it, instead of waking up.

"Lemme sleep," I murmur to the feeling of hands on my body and heat between my thighs.

"Always," the voice close to my ear purrs. "Sleep as much as you want, Quinn."

His words have the effect of dragging out how long it takes for me to wake up. My brain is sluggish to respond to all the perfect, delicious things happening to it. Slow to really come to full wakefulness as Gabriel lazily thrusts into me.

"Gabriel," I murmur, the sound almost as soft as my normal breathing. I can feel more of what's going on this time around. I'm still on my stomach, face against his pillows where I'd fallen asleep. One of my knees has been pushed to the side, and between my thighs I can feel him, warm against my skin while he slides in and out of me.

"Such a heavy sleeper," he purrs, and it sounds like a compliment. "Or maybe you just sleep better when you're in my bed. You're awake just in time, Quinn. Just in time to feel me fill you up again."

I whimper, still half asleep. It's easier now, to just feel him inside me, than to confront the things that I'll have to once I'm awake.

"Relax," he purrs, running a hand down my spine. "You're

fine, darling. Right where you are." I can feel his movements speeding up, and with a jolt I realize I'm incredibly close, like he's been working me up to my release for a while.

He moves to lean over me, dragging my hips up to his so he can sink deeper between my folds, while one hand comes around to play with my clit, begging me to go over this cliff with him.

"Come on my cock while I fill that sweet cunt," he murmurs, and it's all I need to be convinced. I gasp, my orgasm rolling through me so hard that my toes curl. My body shakes, clenching him as he presses into me one more time, his muscles tense as he comes inside of me.

My head spins, drinking in the feeling, and when he slides out of me, I jolt into full wakefulness, a disappointed sigh on my lips.

"I didn't mean to be so asleep," I murmur, sitting up and turning to look at him. "How long have you been back?" While I speak, I rub my eyes with my palms, trying to get my bearings.

"About thirty minutes," he admits, watching me. He's not dressed either, and I pause to admire his body, his face, and everything there is to look at when it comes to Gabriel. "I just couldn't help myself. Do you want to talk about what happened?"

"Sure, *Dr. Brooks*," I yawn, looking for my towel, finally finding it halfway across the room on the floor. "I don't have any clothes," I admit, looking back at him instead.

"I won't hold it against you," Gabriel assures me, a shadow of a grin on his lips.

"I dreamed of Billy earlier tonight. Before Durham called me at the office," I tell him, leaning back against the headboard. He surprises me by following my movement and draping his body over mine, bracketing me on the bed. "I mean, over the past few weeks I've been dreaming of Billy in flashes, but I don't always remember. I think..."Looking away, I frown and some of the trepidation from before comes back. "I think I just killed a man, and I don't feel bad about it. Just like I didn't feel bad about Billy," I say finally, my voice hard-edged. "And I don't know what to do."

He sighs against my throat, kissing the skin there sweetly before biting down. I let him, only letting out a soft sound of enjoyment as he presses my knees open so he can slide between them, bringing his body flush with mine.

"You let me take care of it. Of you," he murmurs. "I've always known you liked killing. I remember Billy. I remember the look on your face, and what you said to me. Do you?"

I think back, dredging up memories I've worked so hard to bury.

"Help me," I repeat, closing my eyes to remember the scene in all its clarity. The darkness had lain so heavily around me back then, and Billy's body hadn't looked real. "Help me, because I'm not sorry."

"And I helped you. Just like I'll *always* help you. There's nothing wrong with not being sorry. Not for you, or me. Not for people like us." He drags me down away from the headboard until I'm flat on the bed again. "And you should stop running away from what you are. Stop pretending to be something you aren't."

"What aren't I?" I whisper in the darkness, the moonlight from the finally clear sky outside illuminating his features harshly. My stomach twists, little butterflies taking off to scramble my insides. I feel almost nauseous, almost dizzy. Yet I've never felt more present.

"You're not *prey*," he growls against my ear. "And you should never act like it again. Do you hear me?" His nails sink into my sides, pulling a hiss from my lips as his mouth works down my neck, to my collarbone.

"You could kill them. Any of them. And you shouldn't feel bad about it. Does the wolf feel bad for the sheep in the field?"

"People aren't sheep," I protest, reaching a hand up to grip his hair when he licks over my nipple.

"Yes, they are, little wolf. They're sheep just waiting for your fangs." He bites down, as if making his point, his other hand coming up to tease and toy with my other nipple. "And you're *mine.*"

"You've said that before," I point out, my head spinning as I jerk his head up so I can meet his eyes. "You keep saying that."

"Well, it wasn't always this true," he taunts, lips inches from mine. "But now you've killed with me. You've *enjoyed* it. You're mine, just as much as I'm yours. And next time we do it, we'll fuck in the blood of our sheep to show everyone else the kind of monsters we are."

"You make us sound awful," I point out dryly. "Like we really are monsters."

Gabriel laughs, though it isn't a happy sound. It's cruel and filled with dark promise, and if I didn't know any better, I'd think he was crazy.

But I know *exactly* what he is.

"We *are* monsters, Quinn," he informs me, nudging my thigh until my leg wraps around his waist and he can rock against my body perfectly. "No matter what we look like to anyone else, we'll always be the monsters that people fear."

I don't know if I believe him. I don't know if I can be the kind of monster he thinks I am. Though when I come again and he drinks in the sound between his lips like a prayer, I start to think that maybe, just possibly, he's right about me.

That he was right all along, and the little lost girl he met in his office was born with murder in her eyes and her heart.

CHAPTER

TWENTY-FIVE

"This is weird," I mutter, letting Gabriel drag me out onto Melinda's patio. "Tell me this isn't weird?"

"It's not weird," he argues. "Come on, how is this weird? Your boss likes you, her husband makes good burgers." He lifts up the burger he's eating and waves to Melinda's husband, who beams and salutes back with the spatula in hand.

"This is weird," I argue, leaning against the tall, sturdy privacy fence as Gabriel joins me. "Are you sure you don't want to, I don't know, go somewhere else?"

"Like my house?"

"Maybe I mean my house," I retort. "You never want to come to my house and have sex. Or shower. Or hang out."

Gabriel rolls his eyes and finishes his burger before turning on me and gently pressing me back into the fence, his body shielding us from Melinda's other guests. His hand slides up my shoulder until he can press his fingers to the base of my throat. "Your house sucks," he tells me sweetly. "It's awful, and that furniture has probably been through six different owners. All my stuff is new. Excuse me if I don't want to get infected by whatever's living under your bed."

"Well, excuse me for *breathing*," I reply, only a little bit offended as my brows jerk upward. "We can't all be world renowned, award-winning sleep psychologists with fancy degrees and a ton of debt."

"Half a ton of debt," he argues. "Closer to a third. You should live with me."

"Yeah? Like your live-in fuck buddy?" I agree, a little aggressively. "The girl you tie to your bed so you can fuck her whenever you want?"

"Like the girl I love," he corrects.

"That's a strong word."

"Only to you. It's the *right* word for me, even though I thought it didn't quite fit before. I was wrong. Come on, Quinn. Don't squirm about it. Just because I haven't said it out loud, are you really so shocked?" He leans in to brush his lips to mine, though I turn my face away, unimpressed.

"You taste like ketchup," I tell him, sneering.

"Then make me taste like *you*," he purrs, and pulls my face back to kill me again with more demand. I give in with a pleased sigh, my tongue finding his before I pull away just enough to nip him.

"Move in because I like you," he insists. "You could just be my sexy roommate if you wanted. I'll make you pay rent and utilities to make you feel better about it."

I scoff and open my mouth, just as a delicate sound of a throat being cleared makes both of us look around.

Melinda stands behind us, beaming, her sister beside her. "I'm so glad the two of you could make it," she announces, handing both of us a glass of wine. "I thought you might not come."

Gabriel and I separate, each of us taking a glass of wine as Marian, Melinda's sister, looks him over.

"It's so nice to see you in the daylight," she tells him shrewdly. "Instead of stalking around her place. He's a good catch," she adds, looking at me and winking. I look away, grimacing in embarrassment at her words.

"Sorry if I've ever bothered you," Gabriel apologizes, having the decency to look sheepish. "It wasn't my intention. Quinn and I just—"

"Say no more," Marian interrupts, flapping her hand at him. "We all have our games, don't we?" She winks at me before walking away to greet someone else, as Melinda stays and sips her wine.

"You'll stay, won't you?" she asks, surprising me with the question.

I look at Gabriel, perplexed, then back at her. "At your party? Not forever, but I doubt he'll let me run away just yet," I reply, putting a small laugh into the words.

But Melinda shakes her head. "Here. In Eddyville. I'm sure the two of you won't stay forever; I'm not asking that. But you're good at your job. You're good at helping, and you know that sometimes help can be unpleasant. I don't want to lose the best social worker I've hired in years."

The praise is unexpected, and I shift uncomfortably on my feet as the feeling goes through me. I don't know how to respond. I'm barely sure what she's asking, and I hope it's not to have a murder buddy going forward.

After all, I'd rather kill people with Gabriel, or not at all.

"I'll stick around for a while, I think," I tell her, a small smile finally curving over my lips. "At least until I've saved enough to buy a better house than his."

"So, forever?" Gabriel murmurs, taking a long drink of his wine while I stare at him flatly. "I keep telling her she could just move in with me," he tells Melinda, who looks impressed. "Then she wouldn't have to spend anything on renting and can save up for a new car."

"My car is fine," I snap, rolling my eyes in his direction.

"Your car has nearly broken down *twice* since you've moved here," he argues, but I shake my head. "You need a new one."

Melinda leaves with a chuckle and a wish for us to have a good weekend, following after her sister as she walks around the pool to talk to the people who have just come in.

"I don't need a new car," I tell Gabriel, sidling closer to him again. "And I don't know if I want to stay here. This place is... weird."

"Not as weird as Springwood." He throws an arm over my shoulders. "I'll do whatever you want to do, Quinn. Stay or go, it's up to you."

"What if I go?" I ask, walking around to the other side of the pool with his body against mine as he falls into step with me. "What if I leave?"

"Then I'll go with you," he murmurs in my ear, kissing me before I can take another step. "That's not a question or a concern, Quinn. It never will be."

I don't reply for a few moments. Instead, I settle against him and take a breath of his sharp, musky scent that I couldn't stand a few months ago.

How things change, I think silently, and drag him down to kiss him once more before we have to go be social.

WHEN GABRIEL WALKS out of his bathroom with only a towel wrapped around his waist and sees what I'm doing, he spares me a glance before he goes to his closet.

"What are you doing?" he asks, looking through a few piles of clothes.

I haven't bothered putting my clothes on. With my knees curled under me, I hold his clawed glove in my hand, running my fingers down one of the blades.

"Thinking," I admit, looking up to watch him drop the towel and drag on a pair of black, loose sweatpants. He sinks down onto the bed, crawling forward until he's right in front of me. "What if I left?" I ask, repeating my question from earlier.

"I already told you, I'll go with you," he replies, reaching out to tug the glove out of my hands so he can use my lap as a pillow instead. He turns his face to kiss my inner thigh, my breath hitching when he does. "I'll go anywhere with you."

"What if..." I trail off, my fingers itching to run through his soft hair. I give in, tugging on it and listening to the soft hiss he makes as the pain catches up to him from my grip. "What if I left without telling you? In my shitty car that you're always complaining about?"

He doesn't respond immediately. He takes a minute to nose my thigh again before sitting up and turning to face me, his body nearly against mine.

"In your shitty car, where I've placed a tracker?" he clarifies, reaching up to wrap his fingers lightly around my throat. His fingers slot under my jaw and he pushes me back, forcing me to sink down onto his bed.

"Yeah," I agree, a grin quick to curl over my features. "That car."

"I'd follow you," he promises, one knee between mine as his grip tightens. "I'd be right on your trail, waiting for you to stop. Waiting to play whatever game you're going for."

He forces my thighs apart around his knee and runs his free hand through my hair.

"Maybe I'll go on a killing spree," I tease, not meaning it. For all I'd enjoyed what I'd done to Durham, and originally what I'd done to Billy, I don't have an itch to kill anyone else.

215

I just know I could do it again without hesitation.

"Maybe I'll clean it all up for you." He leans forward to kiss me, his teeth and lips insistent against mine.

"Maybe I'll let you come with me," I sigh finally, trying to hide my gasps for air after our kiss.

"You're really asking for me to keep you here," Gabriel chuckles, letting me wrap my arms around his shoulders. "You know that?"

"Yeah? Am I?" I taunt, dragging him down to me with my fingers in his hair. "I'd just love to see you *try*." I act like I'm going to kiss him, only to lash out and grip his lower lip between my teeth, a small growl traveling from my lips to his.

He snarls in reply, pulling away just enough to get his mouth free before he licks a line up my jaw. "Poor, sweet, *confused* girl," he taunts, his eyes deepening to a dark, cruel and playful hue. "This is a game you're going to lose, you know."

"Then let's find out," I challenge, pushing against him so I can sit up. "Let's see if you can *make me*."

His next kiss is sweet, the one after it is punishing, and before long I find myself on my back again, with his hands dragging down my body like lines of fire as I close my eyes hard against his enthusiasm.

"I'll never let you go, Quinn," he promises in his soft, rough voice. "Not even in your dreams."

About AJ Merlin

AJ Merlin would rather write epic love stories than live them. I mean, who wants to limit themselves to only falling in love once? She is obsessed with dark fantasy, true crime, and also dogs. From serial killers to voyeurs all the way down to the devil himself, AJ's specialty is in writing irredeemable heroes who somehow still manage to captivate their heroines (and her readers).

Printed in France by Amazon
Brétigny-sur-Orge, FR

14140570R00127